Press Release

From: Max Zirinsky,
To: KSEA Television
Re: Hostage situation at City Hall

This morning at approximately 7:30 a.m., council aide Lorna Sinke was accosted by two armed men posing as police officers at Courage Bay City Hall. When Ms. Sinke attempted to escape, she was pursued by the two men to a second-floor conference room where an early-morning meeting was in progress. At this point, the armed men are holding Ms. Sinke, three city councilors, the district and city attorneys and a judge at gunpoint in the barricaded room.

The Courage Bay SWAT team has secured a four-block area around City Hall. It is imperative that all media representatives stay well back from this area and do *not* interfere with emergency services personnel.

Be aware that the situation at City Hall is extremely volatile. Reports indicate that one of the men is armed with a homemade bomb. SWAT commander Flint Mauro is well-trained to handle the situation. As of today, Anna Carson, formerly a paramedic with the Courage Bay fire department, has joined the team. Carson brings her considerable experience as a SWAT-trained paramedic in Washington, D.C., to this incident.

I will attempt to keep you updated as the morning progresses. It is our goal to defuse this incident with no loss of life. Any media interference will jeopardize that objective and will not be tolerated.

CODE RED

B.J. DANIELS's

life dream was to write books. After a career as an
award-winning newspaper journalist, she wrote and
sold thirty-seven short stories before she finally wrote
her first book. That book, *Odd Man Out*, went on to be
nominated for Best Intrigue for that year. Since then
she has won numerous awards, including a career
achievement award last year for romantic suspense.
This year she has been nominated for another career
achievement award for her series work. She has written
twenty-eight books to date and is hard at work on her
next series, the McCalls of Montana, which begins in
September with *The Cowgirl in Question*. Daniels lives
in Montana with her husband, Parker, three springer
spaniels, Zoey, Scout and Spot, and a temperamental
tomcat named Jeff. When she isn't writing, she
snowboards, camps, boats and plays tennis.

CODE RED

B.J. DANIELS

CROSSFIRE

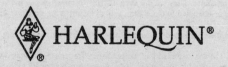

HARLEQUIN®

TORONTO • NEW YORK • LONDON
AMSTERDAM • PARIS • SYDNEY • HAMBURG
STOCKHOLM • ATHENS • TOKYO • MILAN • MADRID
PRAGUE • WARSAW • BUDAPEST • AUCKLAND

HARLEQUIN BOOKS
225 Duncan Mill Road, Don Mills,
Ontario, Canada M3B 3K9

ISBN 0-373-61292-3

CROSSFIRE

Copyright © 2004 by Harlequin Books S.A.

B.J. Daniels is acknowledged as the author of this work

This edition published by arrangement with Harlequin Books S.A.

® and TM are trademarks of the publisher. Trademarks indicated with
® are registered in the United States Patent and Trademark Office, the
Canadian Trade Marks Office and in other countries.

www.eHarlequin.com

Printed in U.S.A.

Dear Reader,

Being a part of the CODE RED series was a thrill for me—and a little frightening. I'd never imagined what it would be like to be in a hostage situation with dangerous men who had nothing to lose.

Being in that room with my characters, I found myself just wanting to get them out of there—and me with them.

I am in awe of SWAT teams everywhere. I admire their commitment and their ability to keep a cool head when everyone around them is losing theirs.

It was a pleasure to be part of such an interesting series with a great bunch of writers.

B.J. Daniels

Many thanks to Twyla Geraci,
who trained to be a SWAT paramedic.
Also, Sergeant Jason Becker with the local SWAT team.
This book is dedicated to you
and the other men and women who risk their lives
every day to keep us safe.

CHAPTER ONE

LEE HARPER was no longer sure he could trust himself. Sometimes he would be in the living room and call to Francine to come see a show on TV. When she didn't respond, he would go looking for her.

And only then would he remember that his wife was dead.

She'd been killed seven weeks ago at the convenience store where she worked part-time. An aftershock from the earthquake had caused the store to collapse. Help hadn't arrived until it was too late to save her.

Knowing all of that, Lee Harper still found himself turning to speak to her and was always shocked and a little disoriented to find her gone. Not that unusual after forty-six years of marriage. No children. Francine had conceived four times, all miscarriages, all heartbreaking. They had stopped trying, stopped talking about children. It was better that way.

He'd been an English professor until last year, when he retired. He could recite complete Shakespeare plays from memory, knew hundreds of poems, and in all those years had never forgotten even one of his students' names.

Until lately.

"It's just grief," friends and colleagues had said. They'd been supportive at first. But as the weeks went by, they suggested he see a doctor.

No one understood that his mind had started to go when Francine was killed.

Now sometimes he left the stove on. Sometimes he didn't know where he was or how he'd gotten there. His grief felt like a tumor inside him, eating him alive, destroying a mind that had once been "sharp as a tack."

For a while the question—when he was thinking straight—had just been what to do. How could he right the terrible wrong of Francine's death? That question had kept him awake for days and left him feeling impotent. There was no way to fix things. No way.

Then he'd met Kenny Reese. And for the first time in weeks, he'd no longer felt confused. Kenny had a plan.

Lee Harper stared down at the crude drawing he'd made of city hall. It was a historic building, U-shaped, one wide marble stairway up the middle, one elevator at the back. For the past week he had staked out the place and knew exactly when everyone arrived each morning and who stopped for lattes and doughnuts, as well as the security system and the exits.

But as he took off his watch and set it next to the blasting cap and explosives, he felt a tremor of doubt. Was this what Francine would have wanted? He no longer knew.

It was the *only* thing he could think to do, and he had to do something. He couldn't explain this urgency in him, a feeling that if he didn't act now, he might not be able to later.

Anyway, the plan was already in place. In a matter of hours it wouldn't be just one old man who mourned Francine Harper's death. When Lee finished, the entire city of Courage Bay, California, would finally feel her loss.

9:50 p.m.

ANNA CARSON lifted the last item from the suitcase. A worn extra-large white T-shirt, the lettering faded almost beyond recognition: Property of Courage Bay Police Department.

Instinctively she brought the soft cloth to her face and sniffed, as if Flint's scent would still be there after five years. Funny, but for a moment, she thought it was. A masculine, clean scent that had always made her heart pound.

She couldn't believe she'd been dragging his old T-shirt around with her all these years. At first, after the breakup, she'd slept in the shirt. It was huge on her, falling past her knees, wide enough for two of her. Just the size of it reminded her of how she'd felt in Flint's arms. Totally wrapped up.

Wishful thinking. And that wasn't like her.

Well, she didn't need the shirt anymore, or the memories, she thought as she glanced out the open patio doors of her new apartment, breathing in the sight and smell of the Pacific. The sea was glassy, golden in the last of the day's light. From the third-story deck, she could hear the waves breaking on the sandy beach. It was one of the reasons she'd taken this apartment. Here she had the view, the sounds and smells of the only place that had ever felt like home.

Too bad everyone in her family had moved away after her parents divorced. Her dad at least was only upstate, a few hours away by plane, in Sacramento. Her mother was in Alabama with her family. Her sister Emily and husband Lance were in Seattle.

It was as though everyone had scattered after Anna left. As if the family had blown apart. Not that it hadn't been ready to blow before Anna had announced that her engagement to Flint was off.

"You didn't really throw the ring at him!" Her sister Emily had given her the eye roll that meant she thought Anna had done something irrational. Her younger sister had been giving her the eye roll for as long as Anna could remember.

"The ring is yours to keep," her mother had said, always the mercenary.

Anna had looked at the two of them as if they'd lost their minds. "I never want to see that ring again. Ever."

Her mother and Emily had exchanged a she-is-never-going-to-get-it look. To them, there was no higher calling than a wedding ring on a woman's finger.

Anna had figured the timing was as good as any to tell them the rest of her news. "I'm going to Washington, D.C., and become a SWAT team paramedic." She was rewarded with gasps from both mother and sister. She'd looked to her dad, expecting his support.

Anna frowned now at the memory. She'd thought he would be excited about her decision.

Instead he'd looked worried and upset. "If you're

certain that's what you want to do," he'd said. "But make sure you're doing this for the right reasons, Anna." Not exactly what she'd been expecting.

"Isn't it…dangerous?" Emily had asked.

"That's what she likes about it," her mother had said. "She wants to turn my hair completely gray." Everything was always about their mother.

Anna shrugged off the past and the memories that had tried to weigh her down the last five years. She wasn't responsible for her parents' divorce—no matter what her sister said.

"You becoming a SWAT whatever was the straw that broke the camel's back," Emily had accused her at the time.

"Thank you, Emily, I really needed that," Anna had replied. "I'm sure it was me and not the fact that our parents have never gotten along, were never compatible in any way, and now, finally free of children, can happily go their separate ways."

"They used to be in love," Emily had said indignantly. "Before…before everything that happened."

Anna turned now to survey her apartment, not surprised that coming back to Courage Bay would stir up the ghosts of her past. The apartment, though, was perfect—small, but the view of the ocean made up for space. She took another deep breath of the night air and let it out slowly. It did feel good to be back.

A tremor of excitement rippled through her. She hugged herself, wrapping her arms around Flint's T-shirt, still in her hands. The excitement was quickly replaced with anxiety. Flint. Eventually she would run into him. He must be a detective by now and on the fast track for the chief of police job. Hadn't that always been his dream?

She wondered how he'd take the news that she was back in town. Unfortunately she didn't have to guess how he would react to her new job. Not that it mattered to her one way or the other. Not anymore.

It probably wouldn't matter to him, either, she realized. Not after five years. Flint was a formidable ghost, one she'd spent years trying to exorcize from her thoughts. She doubted it had taken that long for him to forget her.

Walking to the open deck door, she breathed in the sea air, trying to clear her thoughts. There was nothing more to do tonight. She was moved in and would start work in the morning. She had a 7:30 a.m. meeting with Chief of Police Max Zirinsky.

She doubted she'd be able to sleep a wink, she was so excited. She had the job she'd set out to get. A great apartment. And she was back in Courage Bay. Nothing could spoil it. Not even the thought of Flint Mauro.

She glanced back over her shoulder at the phone book, which she'd left open on the bed. Okay, she hadn't been able to help herself. She'd looked up his number. Just to see if he was even still in town. He was, although he had a different number from the one they'd had when they'd lived together. It seemed he'd moved to the harbor area. She didn't recognize the address, but then, Courage Bay had grown since she'd left.

Anna had made a point of not keeping up with local news during those years she'd been gone. Since her family had moved away, there had been no reason to come back to Courage Bay until this job offer.

For a while after she'd left, she'd stayed in touch with friends in town, but quickly realized she didn't want to know what Flint was doing, didn't want to hear about his latest girlfriend or any stories about his latest case.

For all she knew, Flint could be married by now with a couple of kids.

The pang of regret surprised her. She thought she'd long ago forgotten those silly talks they used to have lying in bed, debating what their babies would look like. They had both wanted a large family. They'd even come up with some names. What was the one that had made them both laugh so hard?

She shook herself out of that thought pattern and closed the deck doors. She had put Flint and Courage Bay behind her. Until Max had called with the job offer and she'd realized there was nothing she wanted more than to come back home. Courage Bay had been her home all but five of her twenty-nine years.

Now she wondered why she hadn't asked Max about Flint when he'd offered her the job. Max had known them both well. He'd known how devastated she'd been when she'd had to break off the engagement and leave.

She guessed the reason she hadn't asked Max was that she didn't want him thinking she was still hung up on Flint Mauro. Because she wasn't. Flint had nothing to do with her life anymore. Nor she with his.

As she turned, she realized she still had his T-shirt in her hands. She walked over to her new wastebasket and dropped the shirt into it. Tomorrow she started her new life in Courage Bay. No regrets. No looking back. She wasn't the same young woman who'd left here, and she was bound and determined to prove it.

10:15 p.m.

FLINT MAURO stood on the stern of the boat he called home and stared out at the Pacific. A cool breeze stirred his thick black hair, lifting it gently from his forehead. He frowned as he took in the familiar horizon.

Do Whatever It Takes. That was his motto, wasn't it? Do Whatever It Takes. And that's what he did every day. Focusing on his job, his boat, his workouts. Not thinking about the past. The past was too painful. And yet it was there. A splinter just under his skin. On nights like tonight he could feel it pricking him, making him itch for something he'd once had—and had lost.

The flag on the bow flapped restlessly in the breeze coming off the sea. He closed his eyes, concentrating on the familiar scents of the ocean and the night. He'd bought the boat and moved aboard five years ago, the only place that he found any peace.

And yet sometimes he thought he smelled her perfume on the sea breeze. On those nights, he would swear that he heard her soft chuckle next to his ear, felt her pass by so close that her skin brushed against his, making him ache with a need that only she could fill. Unfortunately tonight was one of those nights.

Why was he thinking about Anna now? After all this time? He'd jumped right back into dating after she'd broken off their engagement.

"Get back on the horse before you forget how to ride," his friends had advised.

So he'd dated. A lot. But none of the women, no matter how pretty or sweet or capable, was Anna Carson.

"You can't replace cream with water," his boss, Police Chief Max Zirinsky, had said.

"If you're suggesting I was the one who threw out the cream, the cream being Anna, you're wrong. She's the one who broke up with me," Flint had told him. "And don't give me that look. It wasn't my fault."

Max had just shaken his head. "Someday you'll figure it out. I hope."

Max. Flint had a meeting with him first thing in the morning. He knew he wouldn't be able to sleep—not knowing what was waiting for him tomorrow morning at the office. There'd been a rumor going around at work that the chief was going to be making some changes. And just before Flint had left work today, Max had called him into his office.

He and Max had always been close. Not that they didn't disagree at times. Nor did Flint ever forget who was boss.

But when he'd followed Max into his office, Flint had been surprised that the chief had gone behind his desk and immediately begun to busy himself with some papers.

Max didn't look up. Nor did his voice convey any warmth, as if he'd been expecting an argument out of Flint.

"I'd like you at a meeting tomorrow morning. Seven a.m." Max continued sorting the paperwork on his desk.

"Seven a.m.?" Flint asked in surprise.

"Is that a problem?" Max finally looked up.

"No," Flint said quickly, wondering what he'd done that had put Max on edge. "Can't you tell me what this is about?"

"Seven a.m.," Max repeated. "We'll discuss it then."

Flint had wisely left without another word. He knew Max well enough not to argue. At least not all the time. Flint had learned to pick his battles.

Was he looking at a battle in the morning? He had a bad feeling he was. He stared out at the sea, surprised again that his thoughts drifted back to Anna. What was it about tonight? Whatever it was, he'd play hell getting a decent sleep this night.

10:30 p.m.

LORNA SINKE opened a can of cat food and set it on the counter. As soon as she did, the cat jumped up and began eating with enthusiasm. A cat eating on the kitchen counter. Her mother must be rolling over in her grave, Lorna thought with a smile. There'd never been pets in this house. Not while Lorna's parents had been alive, and they'd both lived to their eighties.

"Pets are filthy and messy," her mother used to say. "Who needs them?"

Lorna needed them. She'd spent her whole life in this house with its spotless, lifeless furnishings. It had taken some time after her parents had died, but she'd finally gotten rid of the smell of pine cleaner.

She looked around the kitchen, pleased. The first thing she'd done was strip the curtains from all the windows and discard them. Then she'd painted over the flowered wallpaper. The furniture had had to go, as well. Her father's recliner. Her mother's rocker. She hadn't been able to bear looking at them, thinking she could see her parents' impressions in them, if not their ghosts come back to haunt her.

Lorna opened several more cans of cat food for the other cats and set them on the floor. How odd that her neighbors and some old family friends would think she was lonely in this big old house without her parents.

All those years spent taking care of the two of them. When other women were getting married, having children, making homes for themselves, Lorna Sinke had been nursing her aging parents. The *good* daughter.

And to think that her sister was shocked that their parents had left Lorna the house. Hadn't she earned it? Her younger sister had gotten out as quickly as she could, purposely getting pregnant to escape, Lorna had always suspected.

Well, it was her house now, she thought as she made herself some toast, standing at the kitchen window to butter it and smear a thick layer of jam on it. Her mother would have thought so much jam wasteful. Lorna could feel her mother's disapproval as she ate the toast and stared out into the darkness. She realized that she'd been waiting all those years for her life to begin. Too bad it had taken the deaths of her parents. Not that Lorna hadn't felt a huge weight lifted from her shoulders when they were finally gone.

She shuddered, remembering finding the two of them at the foot of the basement stairs. Her mother must have gone down to the basement for something, fallen and

cried out. It would be just like her father to go down
there instead of calling 911.

Two nasty falls. Both fatal. It hadn't surprised Lorna,
given her father's condition. Couldn't remember anything, even what had happened just moments before.
And her mother, always nagging him to do one thing or
another.

Lorna had warned them both about those basement
steps, but neither of them had ever listened to anything
she had had to say.

She tried not to think about it. Her parents were both
in a better place. She liked to imagine her father float-
ing on a cloud, at peace at last. Her mother was no
doubt making hell more hellish.

Getting out her mother's cookbook, Lorna went to
work making her famous sugar cookies. Her mother
and father had loved them. She'd made the cookies the
night before their fatal falls, putting in her secret ingre-
dient, just like she did tonight.

When the cookies were finished baking, she put them
in an airtight container and set them by the front door
so she wouldn't forget to take them to work, then she
checked her watch.

Time to get to bed. As aide to the city council for
years, she had the run of city hall and she loved it. Hers
was the real power in Courage Bay. Without her, the city
would come to a screeching halt.

She turned out the kitchen light. Tomorrow she could
wear her new blue dress, the one the saleslady said
brought out the blue in her eyes. She wondered if her
favorite councilman would notice.

There was just one fly in the ointment, as her mother used to say. Councilwoman Gwendolyn Clark.

Lorna glanced at the container of cookies by the door. But she planned to take care of that problem tomorrow. Her life was finally going the way it always should have gone, and she wasn't about to let anything—or anybody—mess it up.

10:37 p.m.

KENNY COULDN'T SIT STILL. He paced the trailer feeling as if his skin itched from the inside out. There was only one way to scratch it, but the pills were all gone.

He tried to concentrate on tomorrow. Lottery day, and he was going to be the big winner. All he had to do was to hold it together until then. He knew he'd never be able to sleep tonight. He was too excited at the prospect of being rich.

He picked up the photograph of his sister as he passed the corner table, looking into her face. "It's all going to work out, Patty. Thanks to you."

It was pretty amusing when he thought about it. Even from her grave, his big sis was looking out for him. And to think just days ago he didn't know what he was going to do. He didn't have money to pay his rent, the creditors had been calling every day—that was, until the phone company had disconnected the phone—and there was no one to turn to for help with Patty gone. It had looked as if he'd be out in the street.

And then his luck had changed when he met Lee Harper at that bar near city hall. What a wack job that guy was. Talk about hanging from a slim thread, and to think the guy used to be some well-known professor. Kenny had listened to the guy go on and on about the meeting he'd been to at city hall and how he blamed the city for his wife's death, until finally Kenny had said, "Why don't you do something about it besides cry in your club soda?"

"Like what?"

"Like make the bastards pay for what they did." Pay had been the word that had echoed in his own head. Yeah, *pay*.

"How?"

Kenny gave it a little thought. Hell, people did it all the time on TV. "You could take over city hall, make them sit up and take notice."

Lee perked right up after that.

"But they won't unless you're serious," Kenny pointed out.

"Serious how?"

"Have a weapon or two to hold off the cops until your demands are met," Kenny said, the idea growing on him. Demands. How much money would the city come up with if a wacko had city hall? Better yet, if the wacko had a hostage? A hundred thousand bucks? More?

Lee was crying in his club soda again. "Forcibly take city hall for what purpose besides getting arrested? Anyway, nothing can bring Francine back."

Kenny thought fast. "You said you wanted to make a difference? So you're just going to give up?"

"What choice do I have? I've been to the city council meetings. I'm just one small voice in a city that has too many other problems to care about mine."

"Exactly," Kenny said. "You need to make yourself heard. If you took city hall hostage, you could demand that something be done. Hell, you would be on television. Everyone would know what happened to your wife. The city would have to do something."

"A bit drastic—"

"Seems to me drastic measures are needed," Kenny said, trying to come up with something to appease the old fart. "How else can you be sure that the city won't let something like this happen again? You want your wife's life to count for something, right? Think of the lives you might save."

Lee was looking at him through his wire-rimmed glasses, as if actually considering what Kenny was saying. The guy tended to zone in and out, but Kenny thought he finally had the old fool's attention.

"We both lost someone we loved because of this city, man," Kenny said, realizing when it came down to it, he'd been wronged, too. "We can't just sit back and do nothing." This might actually work. "You want to get the city to listen to you? Stick with me. We'll get their attention all right, man."

"You would support my efforts?" Lee sounded so surprised and touched that Kenny almost laughed.

"Damn straight. You and I are going to teach this city a lesson that won't soon be forgotten." He patted the old man's shoulder. "So do you think you can get yourself some firepower?"

Lee looked vague again, then nodded. "I suppose there is no other way?"

Kenny had shaken his head. "Sometimes you got to

take a stand," he'd said, already seeing how this was going to play out. The city would pay to keep the hostages alive. He'd demand five hundred thousand, a passport and a plane out of the country to some place where he couldn't be extradited, just like the guys did on TV.

But it would only be a ticket for one. The old man wouldn't be coming along. Kenny would make sure of that.

CHAPTER TWO

6:45 a.m. Friday

"Is THE CHIEF IN YET?" Flint Mauro asked as he walked through the employee entrance to the police station.

The desk sergeant looked up and nodded. "Said to tell you to come straight to his office. He's waiting for you."

Flint didn't like the sound of that as he started down the hallway toward the watch commander's office. He was early, but Max was already waiting for him? What the hell was that about? What the hell was any of this about?

Max's door was closed. He tapped lightly.

"Come in," said a gruff, impatient voice.

Flint stepped in, ready to take a good chewing out. He just wished he knew what for. "Chief," he said.

Max motioned him into a chair without even looking up. Flint sat down uneasily and watched as his commander raked a hand through a head of thick, dark hair, then finally leaned back in his chair and looked at him, as if bracing himself for the worst.

At forty-five, the six-foot-two chief of police was as solid as a brick outhouse. He could be tough as nails, and yet normally, humor and compassion shone in his green eyes. Not this morning though.

Flint felt the full weight of his gaze. He waited, growing more worried by the moment. Something had happened, that much was clear. And it wasn't something Flint was going to like.

"Flint, you and I have discussed at length my idea to put a paramedic on the SWAT team," Max said after a moment.

Flint looked at him in surprise. This was what Max wanted to talk about? He relaxed a little. "And you know how I feel about it."

Max sighed. "As you know, we had a court reporter, Lorraine Nelson, who suffered a heart attack during that shooting incident back in September. She lived, but suffered extensive damage to her heart and was forced to retire because of it. If the fire department's paramedics could have gotten to her quicker, maybe she would have had a full recovery. George Yube died after the sniper shot him. Same story there. Had he gotten help faster, he might be alive today." Max took a breath and let it out with a sigh. "The way it is now, we can't get the victims any help until the area is secured. That's not acceptable."

"It's not acceptable to send a paramedic into a dangerous situation until it is secured," Flint said. "Otherwise you're risking the paramedic's life or simply offering the criminals another hostage. The bottom line is, we end up having another person to try to protect, as well as the victims, when our main priority is to stop the bad guy before he hurts anyone else."

"I've taken all that into consideration," Max said.

"Have you forgotten that the last time we let a paramedic in with the team, the paramedic almost got killed?"

"That paramedic wasn't SWAT trained."

Flint shook his head in frustration and shifted in his chair. "Why are we discussing this again? You already know my feelings on this subject and I know yours. How long are we going to debate this?"

Max tented his fingers under his chin, his gaze suddenly steely. "I didn't ask you here to try to convince you. Or to ask for your approval."

Flint felt his heart drop. "I see. Well, if your mind is made up, then why get me in here so damned early?" He swore under his breath as he rose to his feet. "You're obviously moving ahead with this no matter how I feel."

"Sit down, Flint."

Flint dropped back into the chair with a sigh.

"I agree with all your arguments," Max said quietly. "It is a risk, but one that I feel has to be taken for the victim's sake."

There was no talking Max out of this. Flint could see that now. "We have a couple of SWAT members with paramedic training who might be interested in the position, I suppose."

Max shook his head. "I've found a paramedic with SWAT training and experience in situations we've been forced to deal with and some we haven't yet."

"Really?" Flint couldn't hide his surprise. "So when does he start?" He knew his men weren't going to like this any more than he did. This guy better be flat amazing.

There was a knock at the door. Max glanced at his watch. "The new SWAT team paramedic is here now, early, just like you were," Max said with a wry smile as he got to his feet to answer the knock personally.

Flint turned in his chair as Max opened the door. He felt as if a Magnum .45 had been emptied into his chest when he saw the tall, slim figure framed in the doorway. He staggered to his feet, his brain telling him it was a mistake. Dear God, this couldn't be the SWAT team paramedic.

7:15 a.m.

LORNA SINKE LOVED to get to city hall before anyone else. She lived in the older section of town, close enough to city hall that she walked to work. She liked the fresh air, the exercise and the quiet. There were few people on the streets and traffic was light this time of the morning.

She was a creature of habit, leaving her house every weekday morning at the same time. This morning was no different. Only today, she carried more than her usual lunch and thermos of coffee. Today, she had the cookies in the airtight container in her bag. They made a thumping sound as she walked, reminding her of what she planned to do before the day was over.

City hall came into view, the white-stone, three-story building shimmering in the bright blue morning. Lorna always experienced a sense of pride when she saw it. She loved the inside even more, with its ornate moldings and high ceilings.

Some people thought the old city hall building was cold and a waste of space, too much like a tomb, but Lorna loved it. A few years ago there was talk of tearing city hall down and building something modern. Over her dead body, Lorna had declared. After all the years she'd worked here, she felt as if it were her building.

Fortunately the historical society had saved it. Lorna had led the charge—and made a few enemies along the way, including Councilwoman Gwendolyn Clark.

But that was just the tip of the iceberg when it came to her problems with the councilwoman. Gwendolyn Clark was on a mission to get Lorna fired, saying it was time that Lorna retired and the council got some "new blood" in the position. Over Lorna's dead body.

Crossing Washington Avenue, she walked down Robbin Street around to the employee entrance at the rear of city hall. Kitty-corner across the intersection of Bright and 12th streets, she caught a glimpse of the police department. She'd been taken there for questioning after her parents' deaths. The building was new and impersonal, nothing like city hall. She was glad the city had put up a tall oleander hedge along the back of city hall that hid the newer buildings. Especially the police station. The sight of it only brought back bad memories and Lorna Sinke wasn't one to dwell in the past.

As she walked through a narrow entrance in the oleander hedge, she stopped to pick up a candy wrapper someone had irresponsibly dropped. Muttering to herself, she stuffed the candy wrapper into her bag and pulled out the key she kept on her kitten key ring.

Her mind was on the day ahead and the outcome. She felt a ripple of excitement. If this day ended the way she'd planned it, she would be free of Gwendolyn Clark.

As Lorna inserted the key into the lock, she sensed someone approaching from behind but didn't bother to turn around. Blast the woman to hell. Gwendolyn Clark had taken it upon herself to come in at the same time as

Lorna every morning for the past two weeks. The councilwoman was spying on her. Gwendolyn said she was working on a special project. Lorna knew she *was* that special project. The woman was trying to dig up some dirt, something she could use to get rid of Lorna.

It was all she could do not to turn around and hit the woman with the heavy bag. Of course she wouldn't do that. She did her best not to let Gwendolyn see how she felt about her. That alone had become a full-time job and one of the reasons Lorna had decided today she'd do something about the councilwoman.

Lorna turned the key in the lock, planning to say hello to Gwendolyn, pretending, as she had been for weeks, that she didn't suspect what the woman was up to. Today she would be especially nice to her. It would make it easier later this afternoon when Lorna offered her one of her special cookies. If there was one thing Gwendolyn Clark couldn't pass up, it was sweets.

As the door swung open, Lorna plastered a smile on her face and turned, expecting to see Gwendolyn Clark's round, pinched face and disapproving gaze.

To Lorna's surprise, it wasn't Gwendolyn behind her but an elderly police officer, gray-haired, slim, wearing wire-rimmed glasses. He looked familiar. He was hunched over, as if in pain.

"Can you help me?" he said, his voice barely audible.

"Are you sick? Injured?" She fished for her cell phone and had just found it when a thirty-something man appeared from the edge of the oleander hedge along the street. Like the first, he, too, was dressed in a police uniform. But his hair was long and stringy, he'd done a poor job of shaving that morning, and part of his uniform shirt wasn't tucked in. Her gaze caught on his shoes. He wore a pair of worn-out sneakers.

Lorna felt her first real sense of fear. This man, she thought as he ran toward her, was not a policeman. Before she could react, the first man straightened a little, reached out and grabbed her wrist.

She swung her bag with her lunch, the pint-size thermos and the container of cookies in it, catching the older of the two on the side of his head. He yelped and stumbled back, bumping into the disheveled-looking man. Lorna had stepped backward into the building with the swing of her bag. Now she fought to close the door, but the younger man was faster and stronger.

He drove the door back. She turned and ran deeper into the building, her cell phone still in her hand, her fingers punching out 91—

The younger man was on her before she could get out the last number.

7:18 a.m.

ANNA FELT ALL the breath knocked out of her as she looked past Max and saw Flint. She was shocked at how little he had changed. For a moment it was as if the last five years hadn't happened and at any moment he would smile and she would step into his strong arms.

But then she saw his expression, a mixture of anger, bitterness and hurt, assuring her the years had been real, just like her reason for leaving.

His gaze turned colder than even she had expected.

But it was her own reaction that surprised her. She had wondered what it would be like to see him again. She'd told herself she was over Flint Mauro. That there were no feelings left. For the past five years, she'd worked hard to forget him and get on with her life. She thought she'd done just that.

But she'd never expected it would hurt this much just seeing him.

"Anna," Max said warmly. "Flint, Anna is our new SWAT team paramedic. Anna, Flint is our SWAT team commander."

Anna could only stare in disbelief. Flint had always said he was going to be a detective and work his way to chief of police. He wanted to be one of those cops who used his brain instead of brawn, who didn't have a job where he was always in the line of fire.

"I want to be able to come home to my wife and kids at night," he had said. "I don't want to be out there risking my life any more than I have to."

Now he wore SWAT fatigues and a T-shirt with Do Whatever It Takes printed across the chest. What had happened in the last five years to change his mind?

"Please come in and sit down," Max said to her, cutting through her painful memories.

Behind him, Flint was shaking his head. "What the hell? Max, you can't be serious. This isn't going to work."

Max acted as if he hadn't heard him. "Anna, are you all settled in?"

She nodded, afraid she couldn't find her voice to speak.

Flint had turned away, anger in every line of his body. "I can't believe you kept this from me."

"Both of you—sit down," Max ordered.

"Max, I had no idea that Flint was the SWAT commander," Anna finally managed to say.

"Sit."

They sat in the two chairs in front of his desk, neither looking at the other. But Anna couldn't have been more aware of Flint. This close she could smell the light scent of his aftershave, the same kind he'd used when they'd been together. He exuded an energy that seemed to hum in the air around him, that buzzed through her, reminding her of what it was like being in that force field, the excitement, the dynamism.

"One of the reasons I had the two of you come in early is so that we could get this over with," Max said. "Bitch and moan and then get past it. Flint, that's why I didn't tell you until now that I'd hired Anna. I didn't want you stewing for weeks over this. The two of you will be working together. You have the jobs you do because you're the best at what you do."

"Why *Anna?*" Flint demanded as if she wasn't in the room. "Anyone but Anna."

"Excuse me?" she said, turning in her chair to look at him. "Is it possible I qualify for the job?"

Flint shot her a withering look. "I'm sure there are dozens, if not hundreds, of other paramedics who also qualify for the job."

"For the past three years," Max said, an edge to his voice, "Anna has excelled at this position in Washington, D.C., where she was in tougher situations than we've had in Courage Bay. She knows what she's doing and she's damned good at it."

Flint was shaking his head. "Does it matter how I feel about this?"

"No," Max said. "Anna's good and she knows how our SWAT team operates because of her earlier experience as a paramedic with the Courage Bay fire department. She's the perfect person for the job. That's what's important here. Not any petty differences the two of you might have."

"Petty differences?" Flint snapped. "You might remember, Max, we were engaged to be married. Hell, you were going to be my best man. *This* is what tore us apart. Her insisting on endangering herself by training to go in with the SWAT team."

"You endanger yourself with your job every day," Anna pointed out. "I don't see the difference."

"You know damned well what the difference is." Flint swung his gaze from her to Max. "She's a *woman*. She needs to be there for our children."

"You have children?" Max asked.

Flint shook his head in obvious frustration. "You know what I'm saying."

Anna stared at Flint. When she'd first seen him after five years, all those old loving feelings had washed over her like a rogue wave, drowning her in wonderful memories of the two of them together, making her question how she'd ever been able to leave him.

But now as she looked at his obstinate expression, listened to him go on about a woman's place, she knew she'd made the right decision five years ago. The man was from the Stone Age.

"Anna was the best candidate for this job. She can handle it. So don't fight me on this, Flint."

Max turned his attention to her. "Flint has excelled with the SWAT team. He's shown himself a leader. That's how he got the job of commander. There is only one question I want answered here this morning. Can you work together, or are you going to let your differences make it impossible? I have to know right now. Is your past relationship going to interfere with your performance?"

"As you pointed out, we have no relationship anymore," Flint said. "Anna made that quite clear five years ago."

Max shot him a warning look.

"It's not going to be a problem for me," Anna said, sounding more convinced than she was. She'd never dreamed she'd be working so closely with Flint. Was that why Max hadn't told her? "Were you afraid I wouldn't take the job? Is that why you didn't warn me about Flint?"

"Would you have taken the job if I *had* told you?" Max asked her.

Her quick response surprised her. "Yes. This job is what I've wanted from the beginning. I'm not going to let anyone take that from me." She glanced over at Flint. His jaw was set, rock-hard in anger. She knew that look too well. "I have no problem working with Flint. It's been five years. I've moved past all that."

Flint turned his head slowly to look at her and his wounded gaze pierced her heart.

"What about you, Flint?" Max asked.

Flint's dark-eyed gaze was still on her. "Like she said, it's water under the bridge."

Anna heard the bitterness and anger. He hadn't forgiven her for breaking off their engagement. No, she thought, what he hadn't forgiven her for was not being the woman he wanted her to be. And to think she'd almost married the turkey.

"I need a united front here, Flint," Max said.

Flint nodded. "I will treat her like my other SWAT team members. No problem."

Anna recognized that sarcastic tone. Flint would make her life miserable on the team. But she wasn't about to let him run her off. She wanted this job, she'd worked for it, she deserved it.

"I don't want any special treatment," she said, meeting Flint's gaze. "I'm just one of the team."

"You've got it," he said.

Max sighed and got to his feet. "I'm going to leave the two of you alone to talk. Work it out between you. I'm meeting with the rest of the SWAT team in a few minutes. I'll expect the two of you in the briefing room in ten minutes." His gaze fell on Flint. "You're both professionals. Act like it."

Flint grunted.

"That's the attitude," Max said, but he smiled as he came around the desk and put his hand on Flint's shoulder. "It's great to have you on board, Anna. Five years was too long to be away. I'm glad you're home."

7:30 a.m.

THE ROOM SEEMED to shrink the moment Max left it. Flint got to his feet, needing to put distance between himself and Anna. He could smell her shampoo. The same kind she'd used when they'd been together. And her hair was the same: long, shiny, golden brown. Just as it had been the first time he'd seen her.

He'd thought about that day more times than he'd wanted to admit over the years. She'd been walking along the sidewalk by the ball field during one of the police department games. Something about the way she moved had caught his eye. There had been energy in her step. This was a woman who knew who she was and where she was going.

He hadn't been able to take his eyes off her, hoping she would look up. When she did, it had knocked the breath out of him. Her face was striking—the wide, brown eyes, the straight, almost aristocratic nose, the full, sensuous mouth. Her gaze radiated intelligence. Then she'd smiled; a bewildered smile, but still dazzling, blinding, enchanting.

It was as if Cupid had sunk an arrow into his heart. Not that he had ever told his buddies that. They'd have thought him crazy. What? Love at first sight? Get out of here.

He'd been so transfixed he hadn't heard the crack of the bat, hadn't seen the fly ball headed to left field, hadn't seen anything but the woman of his dreams.

He still didn't remember the ball hitting him in the head. He wasn't sure how long he'd been out. But when he opened his eyes, there she was, leaning over him.

"I'm a paramedic," she'd said. "Lie still." She'd gazed into his eyes, so close he could smell her sweet, slightly sweaty scent.

And he'd known this was the woman he was going to marry.

How wrong he'd been, he thought now as he looked

over at Anna. The department's new SWAT team paramedic. Great. He'd spent five years trying like hell to forget her. It could have been fifty years and it wouldn't have made a difference, but now he would be working with her. The woman who'd walked out of his life after throwing his engagement ring at him. And after he'd spent days looking for the perfect ring for the perfect woman. What a fool he'd been.

And nothing had changed. Not his feelings of pain and regret. Not her lack of feelings for him, that was for sure. Except she was back, and now the SWAT team paramedic—the job he'd never wanted her to have.

He looked into her face, searching for some imperfection that would release her hold on him. She wasn't beautiful. Not in the classic sense. She was striking, the kind of woman who made you do a double take when you saw her. A face you never forgot. Imperfect and yet perfect for him in a way that made him ache inside.

The more he'd been around her, the more deeply he'd fallen in love with her. He'd gotten caught up in her enthusiasm for life, her generosity, her sense of humor, her do-or-die attitude. He'd once told her that if he could bottle whatever it was that made her so special, he'd be a millionaire.

"Flint?"

He blinked, so deep in his thoughts he hadn't realized she'd been talking to him.

"I was hoping we could do this in a civilized manner," she said in a calm voice that irritated him more than if she'd sworn at him.

He stared at her. She didn't even seem ruffled. Hell,

maybe she was telling the truth. Maybe she had gotten over him while he'd been wallowing in regret all these years. Maybe he was the biggest fool on the planet. Maybe there was no maybe about it.

"I see no reason why we can't work together, two professionals, just doing our jobs," she said.

He snorted. "You have to be kidding." He was furious at her for walking out on him, for coming back for an even more dangerous job. Didn't she know how impossible this situation was for him? Did she care?

"Why are you doing this?" he demanded. "You know how I felt about you working with the SWAT team. Are you just trying to rub it in my face?"

"That's ridiculous. This has nothing to do with you."

He glared at her. "My mistake."

"You know what I mean."

"No, I don't think I do."

She lifted her chin, stubborn determination in her brown eyes and a coolness that had always brought out heat in him. He'd seen that look way too many times. Unfortunately he could also remember desire in those eyes.

"If you're doing this just to get back at me—"

She laughed and shook her head, eyeing him as if she couldn't believe him. "You haven't changed a bit. You still think everything is about *you*."

"Damn it, Anna, you're wrong. I'm concerned as hell for you. You have no idea what you're up against. I can just imagine what my men are going to think of a paramedic on the team—let alone a woman—let alone you, my ex-fiancée." He tried to imagine this being any worse and couldn't.

"You are underestimating your men," Anna said coolly. "In my experience, the men follow the lead of their commander."

He laughed. She'd just put it all on him. Anna had always been good at turning the tables on him. He glared at her, wanting desperately to take her in his arms and to kiss some sense into her. If only his love for her was enough that he could talk her out of this.

But it hadn't been enough five years ago and it sure as hell meant nothing to her now.

"So, is there a man in your life?" he heard himself ask, and mentally kicked himself.

"I think we should keep our personal lives out of the office," she said.

He wanted to laugh again. "Is that a yes or a no?"

"I've been busy the last five years. I really haven't had time to—" She seemed to catch herself. "What about you?"

He raised an eyebrow. Did she really care one way or the other? "I guess we've both been too busy." He looked into her eyes, searching for just a little of what they'd once had together.

She was the first to drag her gaze away. She brushed a hand through her hair. He couldn't help but remember how her hair had felt in his fingers. He wondered if it would feel the same.

He turned away, unable to look at her as he found himself drowning in memories of the two of them together, laughing late at night, walking the beach as the sun rose over the city, talking for hours on the phone, making love—oh, lordie, yes, making wonderful, passionate love.

"Flint, this has been my life's dream," she said behind him. "This job. I've trained for years for it. Isn't it possible that I just want to help people, that I want to make a difference?"

He felt anger bubble up inside of him as he turned to look at her again. "Being the mother to our children wouldn't have made a difference in the world? No, sorry, that job wasn't exciting enough for you."

"That's a cheap shot even for you," she said. "I was twenty-four years old. I had worked hard to become a paramedic. I wasn't ready to quit a rewarding, exciting job to become a mother yet. But after a while I would have loved to have been the mother of our children. You were the one who said I had to choose. Either I stayed home and started a family right after we were married, or I could pursue a career—without you."

He shook his head. He hadn't meant to take that position. He'd regretted it for years. "We could have worked it out if you'd given us a chance. Instead you threw the engagement ring at me and walked out, left town and obviously never looked back."

"You mean, the way we're working it out now?" she asked with an exasperated sigh.

"Damn it Anna, I know what it was like to grow up without a mother, remember? I didn't want that for my kids. Is that so hard for you to understand?"

"No, but it was all right for their father to be a cop?" She narrowed her gaze at him. "I thought you were going to be a cop who used his brain and wasn't risking his life all the time. What changed?"

He shook his head. "It doesn't matter now, does it.

We have no kids to worry about, and it seems we both think we can take care of ourselves just fine." She was right. They never could have worked it out. He didn't want his wife risking her life at her job. He wanted her at home with their kids.

"Flint, I had hoped you might understand."

He shook his head. "This has to be the worst decision you've ever made, but then, I thought leaving me was the worst, and obviously you've proven me wrong. You seem perfectly happy with your decision."

She raised her chin, that defiant, obstinate look in her eyes. "I am."

"Then we have no problem," he said, and opened the door. "Let's get this over with."

CHAPTER THREE

7:32 a.m. Friday

LEE HARPER had been feeling odd all morning. Now as he glanced around the main floor of city hall, everything had a surreal feel to it. He and Kenny were on the ground floor at the back of city hall and they had their hostage. Kenny's plan had worked.

"Could you help me over here?" Kenny snapped.

He turned to see Kenny wrestling with the woman. Lorna Sinke. That was her name. She was a tiny little thing, thin with brown hair and a small face that made her dark eyes seem larger. He'd seen her when he'd come to the city council meetings. She reminded him of Francine.

"Lee? Could you get your ass over here?"

He shook himself. "Sure." He moved, feeling bulky in the large, cumbersome police jacket.

Kenny had her down on the floor but she was fighting him, kicking, scratching, biting him.

"Get my gun," Kenny ordered. "Shoot the bitch."

"You said no one would get hurt."

"Shoot her, damn it! Or I'll shoot you!"

Lee picked up the assault rifle, which Kenny had

dropped, and walked over to where the two were struggling on the floor. The woman's eyes were on him. She looked more angry than scared.

"Who are you fools?" she cried. "What do you think you're doing? This is a city building on the historic registrar."

"Shut the hell up," Kenny said. "Shoot her, damn it!"

Lee just tapped her with the butt of the rifle, a light tap that connected with her skull. Her eyes rolled back in her head and she quit fighting. "Did I kill her?" he asked, feeling sick and confused. "I didn't mean to kill her." He was having trouble remembering what he was doing here.

Kenny snatched the rifle from him. "I told you to shoot her."

"I don't want anyone to get hurt," Lee said.

"Yeah. Sure. You got the cuffs on you?"

Lee frowned, then felt in the pocket of his large jacket, producing one of a half dozen pairs. He remembered Kenny saying there could be cleaning people or repairmen in the building. Better to be prepared than not. Or maybe he'd said that. Not that it mattered. He handed a set of handcuffs to Kenny.

Kenny was looking oddly at Lee's big police coat. He shook his head and slapped one end of the handcuff on Lorna's wrist. She was coming around, only dazed, not dead. Lee felt a surge of relief. Francine wouldn't like it if anyone got hurt.

Yes, he recalled now. The handcuffs had been his idea. "Easy and faster than rope," he'd told Kenny, who hadn't been that impressed. Kenny had liked it, though, when Lee had told him about the Internet supply shop he'd found where they could get real police handcuffs. "They even have police uniforms and badges."

Kenny had gotten excited then. "Lee, you're a genius. We'll dress as cops. It will make it that much easier to get the old broad to let us in."

"The old broad," as Kenny called her, was wide awake again. Lee could feel her gaze on him as he glanced up. He thought he heard a sound from one of the floors above them. The building should have been empty this time of the morning on a Friday. But he would have sworn he heard a door open upstairs.

7:37 a.m.

LORNA MEMORIZED the men's faces. If she were called in for a lineup, she wanted to identify these two without the slightest hesitation. The younger of the men grabbed her shoulder and tried to flip her over onto her stomach, no doubt so he could cuff her wrists behind her. He appeared to be in his thirties; his face was thin, hair dishwater-blond, and he looked slovenly even in the police uniform. Especially in the scruffy sneakers. He held some sort of assault rifle in his free hand, his fingernails grimy.

"Help me roll this bitch over," he ordered the older one, his breath smelling of garlic and alcohol.

With the handcuff dangling from her wrist, Lorna gripped the canvas bag with her purse, lunch and the cookies inside. Her cell phone was palmed in her other hand where he couldn't see it. She lay perfectly still, hardly breathing as he turned to the other man, the soft-spoken elderly man who'd first approached her.

"Lee? Are you going to help me over here or not?"

Lee was in his late sixties, early seventies, neat as a pin. Even his black lace-up leather dress shoes were shined, creases ironed into his uniform pants. He wore a large, bulky-looking uniform jacket, which, now that she thought about it, was far too heavy for Southern California. He was still kind of slumped over a little, looking uncomfortable, still giving her the impression that he was in pain.

But she thought she remembered where she'd seen him. Wasn't he the man who had come to the council meeting the last two months? Something about his wife.

"Wait a minute," the young one said, straightening as he stared back at the man. "Where the hell is your gun, Lee?"

"You said to bring firepower, Kenny."

"Yeah, so where is your firepower?"

Lee carefully unzipped his coat.

"Holy Mother of— What the hell is that? A bomb, Lee? You got a friggin' bomb taped to your chest?"

"An explosive device, yes," Lee said.

"Why the hell did you do that? Jeez. What if it goes off before you want it to?"

"Little chance of that," the older man said.

"Unless you get shot or fall down?"

"I have to discharge it with this switch," Lee told him, calmly pointing to a hole in the green-colored plastic explosives.

The hole was just large enough for his finger and a small red toggle switch. Lorna knew the switch was attached to a series of colored wires that ran to a digital watch and a blasting cap. She had recently watched a show on TV about bombs, curious how they worked. But she'd decided bombs were messy and too obvious. She preferred a more subtle approach.

Kenny was shaking his head and running his free hand through his hair. "Oh, man, you're crazy, you know that? Beyond postal."

From what Lorna had seen, they both fit in that category.

Kenny was so upset he wasn't paying any attention to her. His kind took one look at her and saw a forty-something old maid, a woman afraid of her shadow, no threat at all.

His kind deserved everything they got.

"Never mind," Kenny said. "I can do this by myself. I don't want you blowing me up because you accidentally flip that damned switch while you're helping me." He put down the rifle, though not within her reach, and turned back around to her on the floor.

As he straddled her and started to reach down to try to roll her over again, she kicked him in the groin.

His knees buckled and she had just enough time to pull her legs to her chest and roll away. Scrambling to her feet, with her bag and the cell phone, the handcuffs still dangling from one wrist, she ran toward the front of the building and the staircase.

Kenny let out a howl that echoed through the rotunda. She raced up the wide central staircase, looking down through the railing only once, with satisfaction, to see that her kick still had Kenny on his knees.

"Get her, damn it!" Kenny wheezed. "Don't just stand there, Lee! Get her!"

Lee was handicapped by the bomb on his chest and his age. Lorna, on the other hand, took all three flights of stairs every day, many times. She hated elevators and closed-in spaces.

She bounded up the stairs. She could hear Lee laboring up the steps behind her. He was breathing heavily and falling behind.

On the second floor she looked up and was shocked to see a group of people coming out of the meeting room, obviously to see what the racket was about. What were *they* doing here? Lorna thought as she recognized three of the city council members: Gwendolyn Clark, Fred Glazeman and James Baker, along with District Attorney Henry Lalane and City Attorney Rob Dayton. A secret meeting?

They all seemed surprised to see her running up the stairs with a handcuff dangling from one wrist.

"What is going on?" Gwendolyn demanded. She was a frumpy matronly type, with a round face and a large mouth that dominated her face. It didn't help that her mouth was usually open.

Lorna could have asked her the same thing, but it seemed pretty obvious. The city councillors were having a "secret" meeting, and there was only one topic Lorna could imagine they would be talking about: her.

"Why is that policeman chasing you, Lorna?"

For just an instant Lorna was too stunned to answer.

Gwendolyn had called a special "secret" meeting with these council members to try to get her fired? Lorna should have known the woman would pull something like this.

Lee's labored steps behind her brought her back to the present problem. "That's not a cop chasing me. He has a bomb taped to his chest. There's another one down below with an assault rifle. They're taking city hall hostage. Get back into the meeting room. Now!"

Lorna herded everyone back down the hall to the meeting room, Gwendolyn arguing all the way. Lorna shoved her into the room after the others, closed the door and locked it. Lee had been only a few yards away. She leaned against the door and looked at the others.

She'd worked hard for these councillors, and here they were, meeting in secret to get rid of her. The traitors. She almost wished she'd left them all outside the door for whatever those two men had planned for them.

Except for Fred, she thought, letting her gaze fall on her favorite councilman. He wasn't like the others. He was kind and intelligent. A nice man. But Lorna knew that Gwendolyn had been trying to turn him against her.

"Barricade the door," Lorna ordered. She'd have to deal with that problem later. Right now, there was something more pressing to take care of. "Barricade the door!"

For a moment no one moved. They all just stared at her as if *she* was the crazy one. D.A. Lalane started to call someone on his cell phone. "Don't touch that cell phone. It might set off the bomb. Barricade the door, then get back from it. The man on the other side of this door has enough explosives taped to him to take out this entire room."

She could hear Lee outside the door, trying the knob, kicking the door, then turning and retreating back down the hall.

Gwendolyn let out a shriek. "Oh, God, we're all going to die." She began to cry loudly. But it got the rest of them moving. D.A. Lalane pocketed his cell phone and ordered the others to help him with the large conference desk. Fred, of course, joined in to help Councilman James Baker and City Attorney Rob Dayton. Gwendolyn stood in the center of the room, wringing her hands and crying.

Lorna's fingers were trembling, but more out of anger than fear as she carefully turned off her own cell phone. Two crazy men had barged their way into her city hall while upstairs a secret meeting had been in session to get rid of her. She didn't know which made her angrier.

The law required all city council meetings to be public—unless the meeting was about personnel. If it had been about city personnel, the city manager would have been here. And since Lorna was the council's only aide and Gwendolyn was dead-set on getting her fired, that definitely narrowed down the agenda of this meeting.

Tossing down her purse and the bag with her lunch and the cookies, Lorna picked up the meeting room phone, hoping the land line wouldn't set off the bomb as she tapped out 911.

7:48 a.m.

KENNY CURSED THE WOMAN who'd kicked him and mentally listed all the things he was going to do to her when he caught her. And he *would* catch her. She couldn't get out of the building and there wasn't anyone around to help her. All he had to do was trap her on one of the upper floors.

He was so sure they were alone in the building that he was startled by the sound of raised voices overhead. A woman let out a shriek. Not the woman who'd kicked him. Then he thought he heard several men's voices. What the hell?

He listened to the sound of voices, then footfalls upstairs, a door slamming, locking. He swore under his breath. Where the hell was Lee? Why hadn't he stopped the woman?

This should have been a piece of cake. They were supposed to overpower the Lorna Sinke woman. Hell, as small and frail-looking as she was, it should have been a cinch.

Once he had a hostage and city hall, Kenny thought he'd be calling the shots. He could hear Lee's arduous footsteps coming back down the stairs. He'd never expected the damned fool to show up wearing a bomb.

As Kenny got to his feet, he told himself that this wasn't going as he'd planned, and it was all that damned Sinke woman's fault. He swore he could hear her upstairs giving orders. The bitch.

He looked up at the sound of Lee's shuffling feet.

"They all went into a room and locked the door," Lee said.

"*They* all?" Kenny demanded.

"I recognized most of them. Three city council members, the district attorney and city attorney." Lee nodded. "I think that was all. I only got a glimpse of them before they closed the door. Ms. Sinke was with them."

Ms. Sinke? Lee was calling the bitch *Ms. Sinke?* Kenny swore. He was going to kill Ms. Sinke. The only good thing was that it sounded like he had some more hostages he could use as leverage. He didn't need Sinke anymore.

As he turned toward the front of city hall and the wide staircase, he heard a sound that made him freeze and the hair stood up on the back of his neck. It was the click of a door opening.

Spinning around, Kenny brought his rifle up, shocked to see that Lee hadn't locked and barricaded the door as Kenny had told him to.

A man in his middle forties, dressed like an undertaker in a dark suit, came walking in with an air about him as if he owned the place. Who in the hell was this? He looked vaguely familiar in a way that made Kenny nervous.

What were all these people doing here?

The man was so preoccupied he didn't see them at first. He stopped when he did, not showing any concern at first to see two policemen in city hall before it opened for the day.

But then his gaze took in the assault rifle in Kenny's hands. Kenny pointed the barrel at the man's chest.

"Well, if it isn't Judge Lawrence Craven," Kenny said, and laughed, finally recognizing him. He looked different without his robe on and that bench in front of him.

Craven studied him for a moment. "Four years for burglary."

Kenny smiled. "You remembered. I'm touched. What the hell are you doing here before city hall opens, anyway?"

Craven glanced toward the stairs but didn't answer.

Obviously he'd come by to see someone, but he didn't want to say who. Now why was that?

Not that it mattered. This was a stroke of luck. "Lee, we just got a real break. This hostage is better than your Ms. Sinke or all the councilmen and lawyers in the world. Make sure no one else can come through that damned door and let's go see what other hostages we have."

7:54 a.m.

AS ANNA WALKED with Flint down the hallway to the briefing room, she couldn't have been more aware of him. After all these years, they were here together. Only not together. Not even close.

When she thought back to when they'd first met... She shook her head. What happened to those two people who were so head-over-heels in love?

She smiled to herself at the memory of the first time he'd asked her for a date. She could practically smell the salt, hear the Pacific breaking on the sandy beach, feel the sun on her back. She'd been coming out of the water, her surfboard tucked under her arm, happy in her element, when she'd seen someone waiting for her.

She'd squinted into the sun, seeing first the dark silhouette of a man, then the uniform. A cop. Her heart sank. Bad news. Something to do with her family?

"Hi," he said. "You probably don't remember me." He seemed so different in the uniform, sand sticking to his freshly polished black cop shoes, and looked as out of place and uncomfortable as anyone she'd ever seen.

"You're a cop," she said, relieved and yet feeling foolish. Of course he was a cop. She knew that. She'd just forgotten that part and hadn't recognized him in uniform for a moment. He hadn't been in Southern California long; his skin was not yet tanned. His hair was straight black. One errant lock hung down over one dark eye.

How could she have forgotten that deep, wonderful voice? Or that boyish face? Or that bump on his forehead?

She reached out to gently touch the knot on his head. "I see some of the swelling has gone down."

He grinned. "You remember me, I guess."

"How could I forget?" she joked, remembering the huge bump he'd gotten on his head from being hit by a fly ball during a cop tournament baseball game, then the crazy ambulance ride to the hospital, where the doctor had assured them both that it was only a slight concussion. And all the time, the guy'd been trying to get her home phone number.

He'd insisted she not leave his side, even with the entire police department baseball team packed into the hospital emergency room, all laughing as Flint pleaded his case for her phone number, saying it was her fault he got hit by that fly ball. If he hadn't been admiring her....

She'd finally given him the number. But he'd never called.

Instead he'd shown up at the beach, and he was so shy, so sincere, so nervous he seemed like a different guy.

"You saved my life," he said.

Right. "It wasn't quite that dramatic."

"You're wrong." He settled those dark eyes on her. "It was for me. It was the luckiest day of my life."

That day at the ballpark he'd been wearing the T-shirt she'd carried around with her for the last five years. His lucky shirt, he used to call it. Lucky because he'd been wearing it the day he met her.

She normally didn't date his type. Jocks. Stars of one sport or another. The kind of guys her sister Emily always dated. And ended up marrying.

Anna had only given him her number that day at the hospital to shut him up. She'd never expected him to call. If he had called, she would have turned him down. And saved them both a lot of grief. Instead he'd shown up at the beach, looking sweet and shy and anxious as he asked her to dinner.

And fool that she'd been, she'd said yes. Look where that had gotten them, she thought now, dragging herself out of the memory as Flint halted at the door to the briefing room.

He opened the door and stood back to let her enter.

"After you," she said. "Just one of the team."

He made a face. "Right." He turned and entered the room ahead of her.

She braced herself. There were always a few men on a SWAT team who had trouble accepting a woman among them. Fortunately most of the men were younger, more in tune with the times. Flint, she hoped, would prove to be the exception rather than the rule, since the Courage Bay SWAT team was all men.

As she stepped into the briefing room, she heard a male voice ask, "You are aware that the last time a paramedic went in with us, she was injured?"

There was some grumbling agreement.

"That's why I've gone with a paramedic with SWAT training *and* experience," Max answered. "Anna can handle herself under pressure. She knows the danger. She's going to surprise you all."

Anna flushed. "Thank you, Chief Zirinsky," she said, moving out from behind Flint to meet a lot of very male faces.

To her surprise, Flint stepped to her side. "Gentlemen, this is Anna Carson, our new SWAT team paramedic. Anna, if you will," he said, giving her the floor.

She looked at the men, then laid it out for them in a flat, no-nonsense account. "I am SWAT trained, second in my class. I spent three years on a Washington, D.C., SWAT team. I received several medals for bravery and dedication to duty. I have been involved in tactical situations from bank robberies and terrorist attacks to domestic disputes and hostage-suicides." She stopped before adding, "I'm honored to be part of your SWAT team, and I look forward to working with all of you."

Silence. Then, "This isn't Washington, D.C. We don't have the same kind of manpower." It was one of the older men. His name tag read T.C. Waters. "I, for one, don't like the idea of a woman on the team. Call me old-fashioned—"

"Old-fashioned and a true chauvinist," Flint said,

and laughed. "Welcome to the twenty-first century, T.C. They're even letting women vote nowadays."

"Aw, T.C. even gripes about women reporters on the field during a football game," a younger SWAT member called from the back.

"Yeah, he says he doesn't like the sound of their voices," said another one. More laughter.

"The bottom line here is that Anna's on the team," Flint said, looking over at her. "We treat her like we would any other team member. Forget she's a woman."

There were some chuckles. "Yeah, right," one of the guys retorted. "At least you could have hired an ugly one, Chief."

Even Max laughed this time. The desk sergeant stuck his head in the doorway. "Chief."

Max went to the door and immediately called Flint over.

Anna didn't have to hear what they were saying. She saw Flint's face, saw the color drain from it and the look he gave her.

His gaze met hers, then moved past to his men. "City hall. Possible hostage situation. Suit up."

CHAPTER FOUR

8:02 a.m.

FLINT KNEW THE DRILL by heart: contain and control. The command center was quickly set up in the briefing room with a view of city hall out the window.

"Lock down that building," he ordered into the high-tech headset that let him communicate with the tactical force.

Behind him, Max was barking out orders, as well. "Get me blueprints. I need an exact location of the meeting rooms on the second floor, all air-conditioning vents and the phone panel."

Techies raced into the room with TV monitors, both visual and audio devices and phone systems. Outside, barricades had gone up and the streets were swarming with firefighters and policemen. An ambulance pulled through the barricade. Just a precaution, he told himself. Just like Anna being here.

He couldn't believe Anna had chosen this day to begin work. All his fears seemed to be coming true. He had to diffuse this situation stat before someone got hurt and Max wanted to send Anna in.

Max pulled him aside, moving the two of them to the

northwest corner of the room to look kitty-corner across the street at city hall. Normally they would have set up the command center across the street from the incident. But with the police station so close, it made sense to set it up here.

From the window Flint had a good view of the right wing and part of the back of the building. The large, old, white-stone building, U-shaped and three stories high, glistened in the sun, the windows like mirrors. Even at this angle, the back employee entrance was partially hidden from view by the oleander hedge. Nothing looked amiss. Nothing gave them any indication that a siege was going on inside.

"I've ordered an evac of the area and the perimeter cleared for four blocks," Max said.

Flint looked at the chief in surprise. "Four blocks?"

"We have the aide to the city council, Lorna Sinke, patched through dispatch. She says one of the subjects has an assault rifle." He met Flint's gaze. "The other has a homemade bomb duct-taped to his chest. I've put the bomb squad on notice. Unknown type."

Flint felt his heart drop. Oh, yeah, Anna had picked one *hell* of a day to start her new job. It would be a miracle if he and his team could defuse this crisis without anyone getting hurt and needing a paramedic.

"Do we have any idea who these guys are or what they want?" Flint asked.

"So far all we know is their names. Kenny and Lee. But Sinke says she thinks Lee's name is Harper. She thinks he's been at the city council meetings the last couple of months talking about the loss of his wife…blames the city. She said she got the impression he wasn't well. We're trying to find out just who all is in the building. Thank God this is happening so early in the morning, but once the media gets wind of it…. I'm going to put Sinke on the speaker phone as soon as the techies get everything hooked up." They would be able to hear her, but Max would talk to her on a private line. "Bradley is out with the flu, the other negotiators are on vacation, so I'm taking this one myself."

Flint glanced over at him, but Max gave no indication he was doing it for any other reason. Like the fact that it was Anna's first day and he wasn't taking any chances because of it.

Sirens blared outside as police and fire departments responded to the call. Fire Chief Dan Egan reported in that he had the four-block area secured.

Overhead came the whoop-whoop of a helicopter taking off from the pad on the roof.

"Building perimeter secure," came the report from one of the tactical teams. "Marksmen observers in place. Tactical team in position. Waiting for orders to breach building."

Flint looked over at Max. Every incident was situational. No one thing was ever the same. That meant each incident was handled differently. Facts were gathered as quickly as possible, then a rational decision was made based on what approach would cost the least number of lives.

There was always a risk. Flint had been in explosive domestic situations that turned violent. He'd confronted armed subjects holed up in alleys, barricaded suicidal subjects and hostage situations involving drunks, crazies, suicidal maniacs with sawed-off shotguns and crying little kids being held by doped-up, drugged-out parents.

Every situation had the potential to blow up in your face at any moment. This one wouldn't have been any different from all the others—if it hadn't been for Anna being here.

Flint looked up, as if sensing her presence. Anna entered the room and came toward them. Five years hadn't dulled his awareness of her any more than it had his feelings.

Their eyes met for a moment, then Anna pulled away. Flint swore under his breath and Max looked up. "Anna, good. I want you in on all of this so we know what we're up against if you have to go in."

Unlike the other SWAT team members now securing the perimeter of city hall, she was dressed in fire department paramedic gear except for the Kevlar vest over her short-sleeved shirt. She carried a jump kit with the basic paramedic supplies and stood, waiting for orders. The hostage takers would think she was just another paramedic. Flint swore under his breath as he realized how vulnerable she would be. This was exactly what he'd feared five years ago.

Max listened to dispatch on his headset, nodding. A frown furrowed his brows increasing Flint's concern.

"Sinke isn't the only civilian in the building," Max said when he got off. "The mayor's out of town, but one of the councilmen home sick with the flu that's going around said there was an early morning meeting to discuss an employee problem. The district attorney was in attendance, as well as the city attorney and three council persons."

"Employee problem?" Flint repeated. "But the council only has one employee directly under them."

Max nodded. "Lorna Sinke."

Flint lifted a brow. A closed meeting to discuss personnel problems, and yet the district attorney was there? What exactly did they have against Sinke, or were they just being cautious?

Max turned to Anna. "So far it sounds as if there is Sinke, two councilmen and a councilwoman, the city attorney and the district attorney in the building. Sinke's got them all in the second-floor meeting room with the door locked and barricaded." He showed both Flint and Anna the position of the meeting room on the map.

The room was at the end of the U-shaped wing with three large old windows along the outer wall. The windows opened, but they were now closed and the blinds drawn. According to Sinke, Councilwoman Gwendolyn Clark said the light bothered her eyes.

"Get Sinke to open the blinds and the windows," Flint said. Max nodded and passed on the message.

Flint's radio beeped in his ear. He listened for a moment, then turned his attention back to Max. "My men are in position. We're ready to lock down the building. Marksmen are positioned in buildings on all sides of city hall. They're just waiting for the word. No sign of the subjects, though."

Flint knew that old building. It was solid, but if the hostage takers wanted into the meeting room badly enough, they would find a way in, one way or another.

He wanted to take city hall before the situation escalated. Before anyone got hurt.

He met Anna's gaze again. Hers was cool, calm and collected. He wondered what she was feeling inside. Hell, he had wondered that for five years, but even looking into her eyes now, he couldn't tell.

"We've got your hookup," one of the techies announced, and pressed the speaker phone button.

Flint heard a female voice. She was talking to someone else in the room. He could hear crying in the background, and male voices trying to soothe the distraught woman.

"Ms. Sinke, this is Chief Zirinsky," Max said on his extension. "Are there any other people in the building that you know of, other than the ones in the meeting room with you now and the two subjects dressed as police officers?"

"Not that I know," she said after conferring with the others. It sounded as if D.A. Lalane tried to take the phone from her, but Lorna was making it clear she was running this show.

"What can you tell us about the two men now in the building?"

She didn't hesitate. "They are both armed. One with what looks like an assault rifle. The other with a homemade bomb. He has it duct-taped to his chest. There is a timer and a switch. He keeps his finger on the switch most of the time."

"What about the men themselves?" Max didn't need to explain to her what he meant.

"They don't know each other very well."

"What makes you say that?"

"The way they act," she said flatly. She described the two men, making Flint shake his head at the extensive descriptions she'd been able to get while facing a man with an assault rifle and another with a homemade bomb duct-taped to his chest.

"Lee's the smart one," she continued. "I remember him from the city council meetings. Lee Harper, that's his name. I remember him now. He's educated, moderate to high income, a retired professor. College English, I think he said at the first meeting he showed up at. That would have been about two months ago. Kenny is a bum, probably has a criminal record. I've never seen him before."

"Think they're related?"

"I don't think so. They don't like each other much, either." A noise. "They're on our floor."

Max looked at Flint, his expression grim. "What was this Lee Harper doing at the city council meeting?" he asked Sinke.

"His wife was killed in the earthquake's aftershock. He wanted the city to make sure their medical response time could be improved."

Max shut off his extension so Sinke couldn't hear. "A bad situation all around, but if we can keep them from getting into that meeting room…. Let's see if we can get to the two of them before they can take the hostages. It's risky, especially with a bomb, but it could get a whole lot riskier once they have hostages."

Flint gave the order. "Breach the building."

"Ms. Sinke? This is Chief Zirinsky again. We're

sending you some help. Please move away from the door, get under desks, anything you can, and wait until you hear our men outside. But stay on the line, if that's possible."

Lorna began giving orders. Flint could hear desks being moved, someone screaming and crying harder, Lorna telling her to shut up, then several male voices arguing.

"Kenny and Lee are outside our door," Lorna said into the phone.

"The SWAT team is coming into the building," Max said, and hung up his phone as he turned to Anna and Flint. "There is something about Sinke you should both know. She would have been prosecuted for killing her elderly parents a while back, but evidence found in her car was ruled inadmissible because the warrant was improperly executed."

Flint couldn't hide his surprise. "What kind of evidence?"

"A drug that was also found in both parents' systems following the autopsies," Max told him.

"And now she's locked in a meeting room with the council members who were in the process of possibly firing her," Anna observed.

"She's had some run-ins with Councilwoman Gwendolyn Clark," Max said. "I guess there is no love lost between them. Gwendolyn has been trying to find some grounds to can her for months, at least that's what the councilman said."

"You think there's some connection between the two armed men who've taken city hall and the special meeting this morning about Sinke?" Flint asked.

"I don't think so, but you never know," he said, and stepped over to talk to one of the techies, leaving Flint alone with Anna.

Flint couldn't bring himself to look at her. He still couldn't believe she was back in Courage Bay. Or why. Sure as hell not for any reason he'd imagined. Or hoped for. Not even close.

ANNA WATCHED FLINT, his eyes hooded, his body tense, facial features a set mask of determination. She braced herself, praying he didn't try to fight her on this, because he would be fighting Max. She didn't want Flint jeopardizing his job because of her, and as stubborn as he was....

But he didn't say a word. He just looked at her, his look saying, "You asked for this."

She raised her chin. Not only had she asked for it, she had trained for it. And she was ready. She had her supplies together and was dressed. The Kevlar vest was cumbersome but essential. At her feet was a jump kit with basic supplies. Now it was just a matter of waiting for instructions, should someone be injured in the breach.

"We were able to reach the mayor," Max said, joining them again. "He confirmed Lee Harper's been coming to the city council meetings. He's the husband of the woman who was killed in that convenience store collapse during the aftershock almost two months ago. His name is Lee Harper, just as Sinke said. He's been demanding that the city do something about its medical response time."

Flint swore. "What's his connection to the other man?"

"We don't know yet."

"They have to have something in common to take over city hall together," Flint said.

Max nodded and turned to Anna. "You ready?"

"Yes, sir."

"Nothing like being thrown right into the fire on your first day." Max studied her for a moment, then handed her a headset. "I knew I hired the right person for the job."

Anna was calm. She'd seen enough of these types of situations to know they often escalated quickly. She didn't think about the danger or what she'd find if she were called inside. All she would concern herself with was the injured and keeping the situation from escalating.

Flint was communicating with the team again. She put on the headset and listened to him work, grudgingly impressed. But then she would have expected nothing less from him.

"No civilians found," came the report. "Floors one and three secured. Something happening on level two."

"Take level two," Flint ordered, and looked up at her.

He would do his job. No matter what. That was Flint. He was tough and determined, seemingly even more tough and determined than he'd been five years ago. But wasn't that strength of mind what she had loved about him? Yes, she thought, but he'd also had another side, a gentle, loving side that had stolen her heart.

"Breaching second floor, all teams on count of three," came a voice over the headset. "One, two, three!"

Anna waited, her heart in her throat. Where were the two armed men? Were they waiting to ambush the team?

Through the speaker phone came Lorna Sinke's voice over the sound of people shouting and a woman crying. "They have Judge Craven."

Judge Craven? There was screaming coming over the phone line from the meeting room.

"Shut her up so I can hear," Lorna ordered.

Max turned to Anna and said, "Judge Craven is Councilwoman Gwendolyn Clark's uncle. What the hell is *he* doing there?"

"Subjects holding gun to civilian's head," came T.C. Waters's voice from the SWAT team. "Please advise."

"Can you get a shot?" Flint asked.

"Negative."

Flint took a breath and looked at Max, who shook his head. "Stand down."

There was shouting in the background, louder crying, then Sinke was back on the phone, her voice tight. "Chief Zirinsky?"

It surprised Anna how little fear she heard in the woman's voice.

"They demand that you call back your men and we open the door or they will kill the judge."

"Don't open the door," Max ordered. There was louder crying in the background, voices arguing, then the sound of something scraping across the floor. "Do not open that door. I repeat. Do not open that door."

"They're breaking down the door!" someone cried above the screams of Gwendolyn Clark.

LORNA WISHED she had a gun so she could shut Gwendolyn Clark up. The councilwoman wouldn't quit screaming and crying. Even when the men had tried to console her. Even when Lorna had threatened to send her out with the crazies.

Now Gwendolyn was hysterical because her uncle, the honorable Judge Lawrence Craven, was going to die if they didn't open the door.

"You hear me in there?" It was Kenny, the craziest of the two crazies. "I'm going to count to three."

After that, things happened so fast, Lorna remembered little of it. Councilman James Baker had his arm around Gwendolyn as she screamed for them to open the door, her makeup running down her chubby cheeks. She looked like hell. Lorna thought about giving her a cookie just to shut her up.

D.A. Henry Lalane, City Attorney Rob Dayton and Councilman Fred Glazeman had all been huddled in the corner, discussing what to do. Lorna had known Fred would be strong in a crisis. He was short with brown hair and eyes, not the kind of man the opposite sex would even notice, much like herself, but there was a kindness in his eyes, a gentleness that made her ache with the desire to put her arms around him.

She'd wondered if he'd even had a chance to notice her new blue dress. Probably not. D.A. Lalane had been talking, but quit in midsentence as she joined them, setting her teeth on edge.

"The chief of police said not to open the door," Lorna told them.

Earlier, the D.A. had tried to take over talking to the

chief. Lorna had refused to give him the phone, and Fred had supported her, saying, "She's doing fine, don't you think, Henry?"

Fred smiled reassuringly at her now, making her feel soft inside.

"We can't keep them out of this room if they decide to come in," Lalane said. "There are only two of them. We might be able to disarm them and put an end to this right now."

Lorna had never liked the D.A. She knew he would have loved to see her behind bars. She knew that he and Gwendolyn were friends. Both of which made him her enemy.

"One of the men is a walking time bomb," Lorna reminded the D.A. "The other has a bomb taped to his chest."

Lalane glared at her as if she hadn't been invited to this discussion. "You know anything about bombs, Lorna? It might not even be a working bomb. He could be bluffing."

"Or it could go off and blow off this part of the building, us with it," she said over the pounding on the door. "The chief of police said not to open the door. He probably knows more about this than you do, Mr. D.A."

Kenny was yelling for them to open the damned door. A second later something large and heavy hit the door. Gwendolyn screamed. The rest of them stepped back, Fred shielding Lorna as he said, "I believe it's about to become a moot point."

The door splintered, the lock broke. The three burst into the room in a blur of confusion, panic and gunfire.

8:32 a.m.

"SHOTS FIRED!" T.C. Waters reported from tactical force. "We have shots fired!"

Flint listened to the pandemonium over the speaker phone. Voices arguing, someone screaming, then the loud thunder of what sounded like a battering ram, wood splintering and shots fired. More shots fired to the sound of screaming.

"Shots fired!" T.C. repeated. "Shots have been fired."

"Tell your men to hold their positions," Max ordered Flint.

"Hold your positions!" Flint said into the headset.

"Lorna? Lorna, are you still there?" Max was calling into the phone.

It wasn't Lorna's voice Flint heard next but a man's he didn't recognize. "She's been shot! We need help! Lorna's been shot and they're—"

A scuffle, a male voice yelling for everyone to get down, more shots. The receiver hit the floor.

In the horrible quiet that followed, Flint glanced up at Anna. He had feared this from the beginning when he'd heard city hall had been taken. Oh, God.

"Who is this?" demanded a rough male voice as the phone was picked up. "Who the hell is this?"

"Chief of Police Max Zirinsky. Who is this?"

"You can call me Kenny," the man said, a cockiness in his tone. "I have your city hall and some of your fine, upstanding citizens, including the infamous Judge Craven."

"I understand Lorna Sinke has been shot," Max said. "How badly is she hurt?"

"I'd say she was toast," Kenny said.

In the background came an older man's voice. "I didn't mean to shoot her. I didn't mean to shoot her."

"Where was she shot?" Max asked.

"In the chest. Now listen to me. If you want to see any of the others alive again, I want five hundred thousand dollars in unmarked bills, a passport and a private jet out of the country."

Max was looking at Anna now, a silent understanding passing between them. A chest wound. Flint swore. She would be going in.

"We need to talk about the injured woman," Max said.

But Kenny was gone, the line suddenly dead.

"I need a clear phone line into that room," Max barked. "Now!"

CHAPTER FIVE

8:47 a.m.

"WHAT ARE YOU DOING?" Lee asked Kenny. When Kenny kept talking on the phone, Lee jerked the phone out of Kenny's hand and turned it off, dropping it on the floor.

"What the hell?" Kenny demanded. "I was talking on that."

Lee looked down at the gun still in his hand. Kenny had shoved it at him right before they'd broken down the door to the room. He didn't remember firing it, didn't remember a lot of things about the morning.

He couldn't be sure what had happened except that there'd been a boom and he'd felt the pistol buck. He'd thought the bullet went wild, hitting high in the wall next to the windows. But it couldn't have, because as the boom echoed through the room, Lorna Sinke clutched her chest and dropped to the floor.

Sinke was on the floor. Lee was still shocked that he'd shot her. He hadn't meant to. The bullet must have ricocheted. He would never have shot her. She reminded him of Francine.

"Is she what this is about?" Kenny grabbed the pistol from him with a look of disgust. Not because Lee had shot the woman, but because he didn't know anything about guns. "If you hadn't shot her, I would have."

Lee stared at Kenny, confused. Had he really just asked for five hundred thousand dollars and a plane? That wasn't the plan. That wasn't the plan at all.

"Why did you change the plan?" Lee asked as Kenny picked up the phone from the floor.

"It was my plan. I can change it anytime I want."

Lee reached up and put his finger against the bomb switch. "We agreed on the plan."

Kenny froze. "Hey, what's the problem here? Let's talk about it, all right? But first, Lee, you need to get everyone handcuffed to the radiators beneath the windows, right?"

Lee glanced at the hostages lined up against the wall by the windows, where Kenny had ordered them. The D.A., the city attorney, one of the councilmen, the judge, the councilwoman. She was bawling and carrying on. The judge was trying to calm her down without calling too much attention to himself.

Lorna Sinke, the council aide, was sprawled on her back on the opposite side of the room. Fred Glazeman, the councilman whose name Lee remembered, knelt at her side, pressing his suit jacket against her chest. The jacket was soaked in blood.

"No one was supposed to get hurt," Lee said, turning back to Kenny.

"Lee, I just knocked down a door. You're the one who pulled the friggin' trigger. How was I supposed to know you didn't know squat about guns, huh? It was an accident. Are you going to cuff the hostages, Lee, or am I going to have to do it?"

Lee looked at the hostages sitting under the windows, but didn't move. "Those weren't the demands we agreed on. You are changing the plan."

"You didn't give me a chance to tell them all of our demands," Kenny said.

Lee was shaking his head.

"Hell, Lee, this isn't rocket science. I'm sorry the woman got hurt, but it was her own fault. Had she opened the door like we said…." Kenny shrugged. "You asked me not to shoot the judge and I didn't—even when you let him get away and run into the room."

Everything had happened so quickly, Lee couldn't be sure how Lorna had been hit. The judge had broken away from him and rushed into the room. There was so much confusion. Lee had watched in horror as the pistol in his hand went off. That's when he'd looked up to see that Lorna had been hit, blood blossoming across her chest as she fell.

He felt sick. This wasn't what he wanted at all. And he didn't want money or a plane or passport. "I have the demands we agreed on in my pocket. I wrote them down so I could read them on television." He reached into his coat pocket. He'd spent most of last night getting the wording right. He looked up, the folded paper in his hand, realizing that Kenny wanted something entirely different and probably had from the beginning. No wonder Kenny had agreed to help him. Kenny was planning to help himself.

Lee felt his finger twitch on the bomb switch, but his gaze strayed from Kenny to the hostages. They shouldn't have to pay because he'd been stupid and let

Kenny talk him into this. His head ached and he suddenly felt very tired.

"I decided to ask for retribution and a new life in another country," Kenny was saying. "That's only a slight change in the plan."

"Money won't bring back Francine." Lee wasn't sure why he bothered to argue the point. Clearly, Kenny had made up his mind a long time ago.

Nervously, Kenny began to swing the assault rifle in his hands. "That's true, Lee. But neither will blowing up this building. You want to have the last word? Then have it on some tropical island drinking fancy cocktails with umbrellas in them. You ever have one of those, Lee?"

"I don't drink alcohol."

"Now, how did I know that? Look, Lee, we need to get these guys handcuffed before anyone else gets hurt, and then we can talk about this. Okay?"

Lee saw the judge look up. He thought he saw something pass between the judge and the district attorney. He knew Kenny was right. If one of the hostages did something stupid like try to rush Kenny, more people could get hurt. "I want to make my own demands."

"You got it," Kenny said affably, his gaze going to the bomb switch and Lee's finger. "So, handcuff these guys and then we'll make our demands, okay?"

Lee saw that the assault rifle was now pointed at him. "Are you going to shoot me, Kenny?"

"Nah, Lee, why would I do that?"

"If you did, the bomb would explode," Lee said quietly. "It would kill a lot of innocent people."

Kenny looked at him as if innocent people were the least of his worries. "I'm not going to shoot you, Lee." He lowered the barrel of the rifle. "But I need you to go along with this. I'm not ready to die. I want Patty's life not to have been wasted. Me dying would just be a waste of two lives, you know what I'm saying?"

Lee just stared at him. He knew exactly what Kenny was saying. His mind was as clear as it had been in weeks.

"Francine doesn't want to see your body blown to bits, either," Kenny said. "Let's ask for money and a passport for you. There's nothing keeping you here. You might as well come with me." Kenny was shifting from one foot to another.

The movement was starting to make Lee sick. He wanted to scream for Kenny to stop. He wanted it all to stop. He hadn't wanted this. No, not like this.

He could feel the switch against the pad of his finger. All he had to do was to move his finger the slightest bit and he would be with Francine. He closed his eyes.

"He's right, Lee."

He opened his eyes to see who had spoken. It was the woman who reminded him of Francine. She was lying on the floor, shot, bleeding. Probably dying. "This isn't what your wife would have wanted. Not the deaths of innocent people."

He liked her voice. It was soft. Like Francine's. Not like that other woman, Gwendolyn. She was crying on the floor by the radiator and the judge. Her voice was like a fingernail scraping down a blackboard.

Lee looked at Kenny. "You can have your money and

your plane. I just want my statement read on the television news like we discussed. Once you are gone, I will release the hostages." As his gaze shifted to Lorna Sinke, he looked into her eyes. One person at least knew he wasn't leaving this building alive.

"Hey, that's cool, man," Kenny said, excited now. "So handcuff everyone and let's make that call."

Was Kenny just trying to get him to let go of the switch? "Here," Lee said, reaching into his pocket with his free hand to give Kenny the ball of metal cuffs. "You cuff them. I'll make sure no one does anything. After all, I have the real firepower, right?"

Kenny tried to hide his anger without much luck. He glared at Lee for a long moment, then slowly he took the handcuffs and walked over to the line of hostages. He carried the assault rifle, all the time keeping an eye on Lee. He was finally forced to put the rifle on the window ledge above the hostages's heads and untangled the handcuffs.

He started with Gwendolyn Clark, snapping a cuff on one wrist, then jerking her back to loop the cuff through the radiator pipe and snap the bracelet on the other wrist.

"No, leave me alone," the councilwoman was crying. "Don't touch me! Someone do something!"

Lee watched Kenny start to cuff the judge and was startled when the desk phone rang. It rang again.

"Answer it," Lorna said impatiently. "I'm sure it's for you."

Lee started to answer the phone, but Kenny pushed him out of the way and picked it up. "Yeah?"

9:11 a.m.

"KENNY?" Max said. Someone was crying in the background. "What's going on?"

"I'm busy," Kenny said.

Something jingled like a chain. "How is Lorna Sinke?"

"How should I know? She's still alive. I don't want to talk about the bitch. How are you coming on my demands?"

Max heard someone protesting in the background.

"Let me handle this," Kenny snapped. "Cuff the rest of them." A louder jingle.

"Maybe we can make a deal," Max said. "I'll do something for you and you release Lorne Sinke so we can get her medical attention."

"Yeah, right. You just hold your breath on that one," Kenny said. "Here's the deal. Either you give me what I want or I kill them all. That's the—"

The sound of a gunshot echoed over the speaker phone, followed by a blood-curdling scream.

"Kenny, did you do that?" Max demanded. A commotion in the background. "Who's been shot?"

"Get me a doctor," Kenny cried, coming back on the line. "You hear me? If you want to see any of these people alive again, get me a friggin' doctor. Now!"

9:23 a.m.

ANNA FELT THE ADRENALINE shoot up, then the calm that always followed. She could hear the confusion in the meeting room at city hall. She desperately needed to get in there. One of the hostages had been shot in the chest and needed medical attention stat.

"Chief, you have to get me in there," Anna said, ignoring the look Flint was giving her.

Max shook his head. "I'm not sending another person in there. If there is any more shooting, I'm calling for a full breach."

"A lot of people could get killed if you do that," she suggested.

"Even more could get killed if I don't," Max said. "This is about preserving life at all costs, Anna, you know that. My SWAT team's lives, as well. The situation is too volatile."

"That's why you need to send me in," she said quietly. "You need someone who can contain that situation."

"And you think you're that person?" Flint asked, shaking his head.

"Yes," she said simply. She had seen his expression when the first shots were fired, when someone had come on the cell phone to say that Lorna Sinke had been shot. A chest wound. "We need to find out what is happening in there before this situation literally blows sky high. He's demanding a doctor. He will let me in. But we have to act quickly."

"We don't even know who shot Kenny," Flint pointed out. "Who else has a gun in there besides Kenny and Lee?"

"One of the councilmen?" Max suggested, then swore under his breath. "It's turning into a free-for-all." He glanced at Anna, then picked up the phone again. "What is the extent of your injuries?" Max asked Kenny.

B.J. DANIELS   79

"My arm. God, it hurts like hell. Get me a doctor, damn it. Now! Or I'm going to start killing everyone in this room, you hear me? Just the doctor. No one else comes in. You hear?"

"I'm getting you someone, but I need you to assure me that she will be safe," Max said.

"*She?* You can't find a *male* doctor?" Kenny cried.

"Not on short notice."

Kenny was swearing profusely. "Send the bitch in."

Flint raked a hand through his hair and shook his head at Anna.

The more they learned about Kenny, the more dangerous this situation became. Anna could understand Flint's concern.

"How is Lorne Sinke doing?" Max asked Kenny.

"How the hell should I know?" came the reply.

Max hung up the phone and looked at Anna. "I can't send you in there. It's just too dangerous. I'm not giving this guy another hostage."

"What about the wounded hostage, Max?"

He shook his head as one of the techs motioned that he had an outside call. He went to take it.

Flint looked relieved but equally worried about the hostages. This situation could blow at any time.

Max returned a few moments later. "That was the police commissioner and the governor on a conference call. Judge Craven is involved in some sensitive cases that the state doesn't want to lose. The police commissioner and governor want us to handle this as quickly and discreetly as possible. They don't want anything to happen to Judge Craven."

Flint shook his head. "Politics! What about the other hostages?"

Max shot him a look. "Don't preach to the choir, Flint."

"Well, Anna isn't going in there alone," Flint said, a finality in his voice that made even Max raise a brow. "I don't want her to go in at all, but I know there is no stopping her."

"Kenny is allowing only one person in and only because he's injured," Max explained quietly, calmly. "Anna might be just the person we need in there. She might be able to defuse the situation."

"Or get herself killed," Flint said. "I'll go. Tell Kenny you found a male doctor."

"It's a chest wound," Anna said. "You don't have the training. I do. Stop arguing and tell me how I can help once I'm inside."

"You don't even know if he will let you work on Lorna Sinke when you get in there," Flint told her. "He's been shot. But once you fix him up, you'll just be another hostage. He won't let you leave."

No one argued that point. They couldn't depend on Kenny to keep any of his promises. Quite the opposite.

"All your experience aside," Flint said. "You have no idea what you're walking into this time."

"We seldom do," she said.

"This is what she's been trained for," Max said. "Once she's inside and has stabilized the victim, she can use her SWAT training to help contain and control the situation."

Max turned to Anna. "We have marksmen observers

on the roof across the street in the law offices." He rolled out the map of the second floor of city hall.

"The problem is the guy with the bomb," Flint said. "We can't take a shot if there is any chance Lee Harper really did build a working bomb."

Max nodded. "That's why I need someone to get a good look at the bomb." He glanced at Flint. "I need that audio and visual to that meeting room."

"My men tried to get it in," Flint told him. "But the building is old and every sound echoes. They can't do it without being detected unless there is enough noise in the meeting room to cover the sounds."

"Like during the commotion when everyone is watching the door as they're letting me into the room," Anna said, looking at Flint, knowing that was what he was getting at. It surprised her. There had to be more to his plan, since he'd already said he wasn't letting her go in there alone.

"We can't risk having one of the marksmen take out either of the subjects until we can verify the status on that bomb," Max said, looking over at Anna. "I'm going to need you to get a good look at the device. You'll have to pass a signal. One hand, five fingers splayed and held up, is a yes, it's a bomb. Ten fingers, both hands, fingers splayed, is a no, period. If we can't get the visual in through the vents, you'll have to go to the window. Can you do that?"

She nodded.

Flint was shaking his head.

"I'll see what I can do," she said. "The way Lorna described the man with the bomb, I think I might be able to talk him down. Get me everything you have on his wife and the accident."

Max met her gaze with approval. "You got it." He turned to one of his men and gave the order.

"She can't send a detailed diagram of a bomb with a yes or no," Flint said when Max was finished. "Even if you get visual through the vents, it won't be clear enough for us to know how to disarm that bomb."

"Flint—"

"I'm not saying that Anna can't pull this off. I don't doubt she can do anything she sets her mind to." He glanced at her, a half smile curling his lips. "I've seen her determination." He swung his gaze back to Max. "But I might be able to *disarm* that bomb. If I can't, I can make sure that bomb doesn't go off in that room with all those hostages. Anna can't do that. You need me in there and you have just the opportunity to get me inside. Tell him you've found a male doctor."

Anna started to remind him again that he didn't have the medical experience.

"Your other option is to take the chance with Anna and all those hostages," Flint said. "What if it really is a bomb and Anna can't talk him down?" Flint shook his head. "Tell him you found a male doctor—and a nurse." He looked over at Anna. "Anna and I will both go in."

Anna saw where he was headed with this. "The doctor needs a nurse to help him. Kenny is obviously a bigger chauvinist than Flint. He'll expect a nurse to do the dirty work while the doctor saves his life."

Flint actually smiled. "I love it when we're on the same wavelength." His smile faded as he obviously realized what he'd said. "Max, you have to talk Kenny into letting us both come in. Look how quickly things have escalated in that room. You know it will only get worse if you don't send in a doctor. If you breach now, he'll try to kill as many people as he can."

Max sighed as the phone began to ring. Kenny calling back. He picked up after four rings.

"You'd better be getting me a doctor in here and now," Kenny cried. "I'm going to finish off the one bitch, then kill the other one unless there is a doctor here in fifteen minutes. You got fifteen minutes, you hear me?" The connection was broken with the sound of Kenny slamming down the phone.

"I'm not sure we shouldn't go full breach and take our chances," Max said.

Flint frowned. "You could lose everything, including the judge and part of the building. You aren't going to do that."

"I don't want to lose you and Anna, either," Max snapped. "You are no doctor, Flint. If Kenny figures that out, he'll kill both of you."

"Don't you think I know that?" Flint looked over at Anna. "Anna's going to make me look good. She can tell me everything I need to do, and if I fumble, I can call her over to help me. If the guy is just shot in the arm…"

"He's right, Max. I can talk him through it. I'll get him to stall as much as he can to give me time to work on Lorna Sinke…if she's still alive by the time we get in there."

"Send us in. Anna and I are the best bet you have to end this without a lot of bloodshed. If you go full breach," Flint added, "you know he'll kill as many people as he can before you can get into that room, even if the other guy doesn't blow everyone to kingdom come."

Max looked from Flint to Anna, then nodded. "I'll try to talk Kenny into it. But if I can't, we're going full breach. Anna isn't going in there alone."

"That is something we can agree on," Flint said.

Anna watched Max pick up the phone, knowing that if something happened to Judge Craven, it would mean the end of Max's career. And probably Flint's, as well. She turned away, settling her gaze on Flint. "Tell me you aren't doing this to try to protect me."

He gave her a look. "You're just one of the SWAT team, sweetheart. I wouldn't let any of my men go in there alone."

"I hope you mean that. You know how I feel about this," she said.

His jaw muscle tightened, his eyes dark. "You've been abundantly clear about everything, especially how you feel."

What a lie that was, she thought. Even *she* didn't know how she felt about this man right at this moment. Seeing Flint again had made her feel things she'd thought long dead and buried. He made her think about the past, about the two of them and their dreams and plans. True, their reasons for breaking up five years ago hadn't changed. But the feelings were still there, feelings she had denied until today.

Of course, she wasn't about to tell Flint that. This situation was bad enough as it was. If she wanted to be treated like one of the SWAT team, then telling him she still felt something for him was definitely out.

Anyway, by the time this was over, all of Flint's male chauvinistic bias would have come out again and she probably wouldn't be able to stand the sight of him.

He was nice to look at right now, though. Dark in a very intense sort of way that made any woman still breathing notice him. Anna was no exception. She wondered if Flint had been honest about being too busy the past five years to get serious about anyone.

She told herself she was only thinking about this to keep her mind off what was really going on in city hall. She'd always prided herself on her cool, calm and collected demeanor while under the gun. Today was no different from any other on the job, she told herself. She couldn't let even the thought of Flint change that.

"I've found you a male doctor," Max was saying on the phone with Kenny. "But he won't come in without his nurse."

"What?" Kenny bellowed. "His nurse? I don't give a damn if he brings his wife, as long as he gets in here."

Max looked at Flint and nodded. "But I will need the release of one hostage for the doctor."

"Listen, you—"

"It's the way it's done," Max said. "I know you've seen enough of these kinds of shows on television and you're a smart man. I'm trying to work with you, but I'm not the last word here."

Kenny was grumbling but obviously coming around. "One hostage. I have just the one in mind. The sniveling, crying one." Gwendolyn Clark.

"I was thinking the injured one," Max said. "We need to get her to a hospital."

"No way, that bitch isn't going anywhere," Kenny snapped.

Max continued to negotiate, but one thing was definite: Flint and Anna were going into what they would call an explosive situation—if they were alive later to joke about the danger.

"You'll need to change into Courage Bay Fire Department paramedic clothing," Anna said to Flint. "With you going in, too, we can take more oxygen for the chest wound victim and extra bandages."

FLINT LOOKED AT HER, realizing what he'd done. He was going into that situation with her, and even if he admitted she was right and the only reason he'd done it was to try to protect her, he was smart enough to know how impossible that was going to be. They were walking into a potentially lethal situation unarmed.

This was Anna's dream job? And at one time he'd wanted to have babies with this obviously demented woman.

He watched her make a call for the supplies they would need.

"Flint?" she said as she hung up. "I have a paramedic uniform coming for you. I think that will be better than street clothes. Definitely better than your SWAT gear. And extra oxygen is coming in by helicopter."

He nodded. All he could be thankful for right now was that he was going in with her. Just the thought of her going into that room alone… And while Max had said he wouldn't send Anna in, Flint knew she would have eventually worn him down and gone in alone if he hadn't come up with a plan. He knew Anna. Oh, God, how he knew her. "Anna, please reconsider—"

"Don't try to stop me," she said. "Just let me do my job."

He heard the plea in her tone. He nodded. "Just tell me what you suggest I do once we're inside."

She nodded. "Just remember you're a doctor. Look...smart." She actually smiled at that. "If you get in trouble, ask for my help. But try to give me time to stabilize Lorna." She didn't say, "If Lorna is still alive" again, but the words hung in the air between them. They might be going in too late for the council's aide.

"Just follow my lead," Anna continued. "You check his wound, frown a lot, convince him he needs to be at the hospital if possible. If it's just a flesh wound, cut away any cloth, stop the bleeding with four-by-four trauma dressing and then take your time bandaging him up."

Flint nodded. "I need to get a good look at that bomb."

"I'll do what I can to help you," she said.

He smiled then, remembering how good they used to be together. He'd missed her, missed those late-night meals they used to whip up in his kitchen, missed after dinner, lying on the couch in each other's arms. Yeah, they used to work together well.

"We always did make a hell of a team," he said, and smiled at her, knowing there was no changing this woman's mind. "We used to say it was magic, whatever it was between us."

Her gaze seemed to soften. "We can do this, if anyone can."

He nodded. That was just it. He wasn't sure anyone

could stop the two hostage takers from what they planned to do. He looked away, not wanting her to see how worried he was. It made him sick at just the thought of the danger she would be in. Didn't she realize this was killing him?

He fought the urge to reach out and brush his fingers across her cheek. He wanted to touch her, to assure himself that she was real. He didn't want to consider that if he did touch her, it might be the last time.

They were going to need all the magic they could make together today.

Max joined them again, his gaze taking in the two of them. He frowned. "Everything all right between the two of you?"

"Fine," Flint said. "We're ready."

Max looked at Anna. She nodded.

"He's agreed to let the male doctor and his nurse in. He sounds like he's in pain, but not critical." Max glanced at Flint. "He's right on the edge, Flint."

Flint heard the hesitancy in the chief's voice and knew what was coming, but not how to stop it.

"You're all wrong for the role of the doctor, Flint," Max said. "I'm afraid you'll only make things escalate in there once they see you. Someone other than you needs to go in."

Flint started to argue but Anna cut him off.

"You're right, Max. Flint looks too much like a cop, but I have an idea." Anna could see that Flint was treading on thin ice with his job because of her. She hadn't wanted this, but she understood Max's reservations. Flint was a large man and in obvious good shape. He didn't look like a doctor. Nor would he be able to perform like one once they were inside.

But there was no one she trusted more to go in there with her. He was right, the two of them had made one hell of a team. She trusted him with her life. And even more important, he could trust her with his.

"The problem, Flint, is that you look too tough," she said to him. "Max, we need a metal leg brace." She met Flint's gaze. "You have a bum leg, a *bad* limp—something that weakens you in their eyes."

Max nodded, smiling as he turned to one of his men. "Find us a leg brace that will fit Flint. Hurry. Good thinking, Anna."

Flint gave her a nod. "Nice work."

She wasn't sure he was sincere but it didn't matter. She just might have saved his job. She prayed it wouldn't come down to her having to save his life.

"Can we get any kind of weapon into the brace?" Flint asked.

Max was shaking his head. "Too risky. I'd like to send in a radio, but if they search your bag, which I'm sure they will, we don't want them to know everything we're doing by stumbling onto our channel. But I do have something for Anna." He motioned to a techie, who handed him a device that looked like a hearing aid. "Here, put this in your ear behind your long hair. You won't be able to communicate with us, but we can at least talk to you."

She nodded and inserted the device in her ear, then covered it with her hair.

"You realize if they find it on her they'll be able to hear, as well," Flint said.

"That's why I need that audio and visual in the room," Max said.

Flint nodded. "We'll make as much noise as possible when we go in. Have the team try to put in the audio and visual receivers then. If they succeed, watch me for the same signals you gave Anna, five fingers being yes, ten, no. If we need you to go full breach, I'll give you a count of five, one finger to start the five-minute count."

"If things get out of control, I'll warn Anna before we go full breach. You know what to do with the guy wearing the bomb if that happens. No heroics. Sometimes you have to sacrifice a life for the good of the rest."

Flint nodded solemnly. He knew what to do. Take out Lee Harper. He was not to attempt to disarm the bomb if it would jeopardize himself or Anna or the hostages or even the other hostage taker. The area beneath the second-story windows had been cleared. If things went badly, Flint was to send Lee and the bomb out the window.

"I hope to hell it doesn't come to that," Max said.

"Me, too." Flint looked at Anna. "Me, too."

CHAPTER SIX

9:29 a.m.

LEE LISTENED TO Kenny yelling, "Someone shot me! Who the hell shot me?" Kenny had slid down onto the floor by the phone, holding his arm, cursing and glaring at the hostages as if thinking of turning the assault rifle on the whole bunch.

Lee knew he couldn't let Kenny do that. But stopping Kenny was proving to be a problem. Lee was too old and no physical match for Kenny. His only weapon was the bomb, literally, and while it made a good threat, the reality was flipping the switch and killing everyone. He'd already shot poor Lorna Sinke. He didn't want any more bloodshed. If he could prevent it.

Lee swung his gaze over the hostages, trying to understand where the shot had come from. The blinds were down, but he could see the windows were all intact, so it hadn't been a sharpshooter from one of the other buildings or one of the helicopters that had been circling outside.

He looked up. No holes in the ceiling. The shot had to have come from inside this room. And yet none of the hostages appeared to have a gun.

Lee stared at Lorna Sinke lying in a pool of her own blood. Councilman Fred Glazeman was bending over her, pressing his good suit jacket to the wound. Neither seemed interested in what was happening on Kenny's side of the room.

"Damn it, *now* will you get the rest of them handcuffed to the radiator pipes?" Kenny was yelling at Lee. Councilwoman Gwendolyn Clark was crying hysterically. "One of those sons of bitches shot me. Find the gun."

Lee moved across the room to where Kenny had dropped the last two pairs of cuffs when he'd gone to answer the phone. Lee picked up the handcuffs with his free hand, keeping his gaze on the hostages, his finger on the bomb toggle switch.

One of them had to have shot Kenny. He cuffed the district attorney, then the judge, and searched them all. "I didn't find a gun."

"What about them?" Kenny cried, indicating Lorna Sinke and Fred Glazeman.

Lee shuffled over to them. He felt exhausted, his head was hurting. He hated getting old. He used to have so much energy. Now any little thing wore him out. And he hadn't slept very well last night. Plus, he couldn't remember spending this much time on his feet lately.

Being careful not to disturb the suit jacket soaked with the woman's blood, he searched the two of them with his free hand. The other hand stayed on the bomb switch. Then he turned to shake his head at Kenny.

"Maybe he shot himself," Lorna suggested in a whisper.

More and more the woman reminded him of Francine, Lee thought as he looked down at her and saw the slight smile on her lips. A strong woman, he thought. Wounded, probably dying, and still she had a sense of humor. Francine had been like that.

"Damn it, Lee, what are you doing?" Kenny demanded.

Lee turned to look at him. Kenny was sprawled on the floor, his back to the wall, the assault rifle in his lap, blood seeping out from between his fingers as he squeezed his upper arm in obvious pain.

The thought surprised Lee, but he wished he had the handgun Kenny had given him earlier. Even after accidentally shooting Lorna Sinke, Lee wouldn't have minded having the gun in his hand again. Only this time, he would have used it on Kenny. He would have walked right over to him and shot him between the eyes and ended this the way it was supposed to have ended.

Kenny was trying to turn what was to have been a statement into something else, something crass and crude. Francine definitely wouldn't have liked it.

"Shut up!" Kenny yelled at the hysterical councilwoman. "Shut her up or I swear…"

The judge was trying to reason with Gwendolyn.

Lee looked down at the bomb, at the tiny red switch. He could end this in an instant. End it all. And take Kenny with him.

But then he looked at the woman on the floor again, the woman who reminded him of Francine.

"No one was supposed to get hurt," Lee said, more to himself than her. She didn't say anything. But Kenny overheard.

"*I* got hurt," Kenny bellowed. "If you had gotten them handcuffed like I told you... Find that damned gun. Find the bastard who shot me. I'll kill them all if you don't."

Lee couldn't let Kenny do that. Maybe once Kenny got the money and the plane... But Lee knew the city wasn't going to give Kenny Reese anything except a pauper's burial when this was all over. If there was enough of Kenny left to bury.

As Lee looked again at the hostages, he noticed something he hadn't seen before the shot was fired. Behind the blinds, one of the large old windows was open a crack—wide enough to get rid of a handgun.

He studied the faces of the hostages, knowing that they would never tell who'd fired the shot even if one of them had seen it. The shooter must have gotten rid of the gun during the confusion after Kenny was shot.

"If you can't get them all handcuffed," Kenny said, "I can just shoot them."

Lee felt light-headed. Clearly, Kenny wanted to kill someone. He didn't care whom. "I'm sorry, but you'll have to go over with the others," Lee said to Councilman Glazeman, who was still beside the council's aide. Fred continued to hold the woman's hand and press his jacket to her wound. There was an awful lot of blood.

"She needs medical attention," Fred whispered so Kenny wouldn't hear.

Lee remembered that Fred had been genuinely compassionate when Lee had told him at the council meetings about Francine and how he felt the city needed to do something about what had happened. The other councillors had treated him like an addled old man.

"Someone has to keep this pressed to her chest," Fred said.

"If you can't get him handcuffed to a radiator soon, Lee, I'm going to shoot him," Kenny hollered.

Lee looked at Fred. "Please," he whispered. "I don't want you to get hurt."

"It's all right," Lorna said. "I can hold the jacket on the wound." She placed her hand over Fred's and slowly he pulled his bloody hand free and moved to the radiator against the wall. Lee took the cuff off Lorna's wrist, the last handcuff he had, and walked over to the outside wall to attach one end to Fred's wrist, the other to the pipe. He didn't think Kenny would notice that he hadn't cuffed both of the man's hands around the pipe the way he had with the others. It was the one kindness he could show the man who had been kind to him.

"What about her?" Kenny demanded, motioning toward Lorna.

"I don't have another pair of cuffs," Lee said. "It isn't as though she's going anywhere."

"Maybe next time she'll shoot *you,*" Kenny said, looking at her as if he wouldn't be surprised if she was the one who'd shot him.

"She doesn't have a gun." Lee glanced down at Lorna. She had closed her eyes. He just hoped she wasn't dead. He also hoped she wouldn't turn out to be the one who'd shot Kenny. Lee knew he wouldn't be able to save her if Kenny found out.

"I'm really sorry I shot you," he whispered to Lorna. She didn't open her eyes.

When he turned, he saw that Kenny had forgotten about

Lorna and the gun. He was grimacing in pain and staring at his bleeding arm. "Where the hell is that doctor?"

10:37 a.m.

FLINT LEAD THE WAY to the ambulance parked behind the police station. He and Anna had gone out the back and would backtrack a few blocks before turning on the siren and racing toward city hall—just in case the hostage takers were watching from the window.

Flint could see how anxious Anna was to get there. He just hoped the injured woman hung on long enough for them to get inside the building—and to get her and Anna out again.

That would be the first step, to get the injured woman and Anna out and size up the situation. First, he would determine whether or not they were dealing with a live bomb. Then he would see how many other weapons were involved, make an evaluation of the two men and decide his next course of action.

He took a seat in the back of the ambulance across from Anna, the medical bags between them. He would have to take his lead from Anna when it came to the medical part of the mission. He'd had a little paramedic training, but Anna would be calling the shots. Nothing new there, he thought. She'd been calling the shots for years.

"Once we get inside, stop the bleeding first," Anna repeated. "Take your time. He won't notice that I'm working on the woman as long as you're busy with him."

Flint nodded. She didn't seem nervous, just anxious to get to work. He would have gladly given his life twice over to keep her out of that building. But the best he could do was to try to protect her once they were inside.

Without thinking, he reached over to tuck a lock of her hair behind her ear. Her hair felt exactly as he remembered it, and he knew if he took her in his arms and kissed her, it would be like the first time—the night of their first date.

He'd taken her to his favorite restaurant, a small seafood place on the beach. They'd sat at a table looking out over the water, the warm sea breeze stirring her hair, the sound of the sea beneath them. He remembered the way the candlelight flickered in the breeze, the light played on her face. God, she was beautiful that night.

He had stared at her, watching her talk, watching the way her lips moved, thinking how badly he wanted to kiss her. He'd known she hadn't been so sure about going out with him. He'd feared it was because he was a cop.

"I had an uncle who was a cop," she'd said, and he'd sensed there was something there, something painful.

He hadn't pried, sensing that she didn't want to tell him. He later learned that her uncle had been killed in the line of duty. He'd changed the subject, asking her about Courage Bay. He'd been on the city's police force for only a few weeks, the same amount of time he'd been in Southern California, but he liked it here more and more, he'd thought, looking at her.

She was smart and funny and he'd known he had to see her again. But he'd also sensed he needed to take it slow—the very last thing he'd wanted to do.

When they'd finished dinner, they'd gone for a walk on the beach. She'd insisted he take off his shoes and roll up his pant legs. "You have to feel the sand between your toes," she'd said, laughing at how white his feet were.

She had pulled off her shoes, then taken off down the beach, splashing in the shallow water as she ran, the moonlight turning her hair to gold, the sound of the surf mixing with her laughter, her footprints washing away behind her.

He'd run after her, catching her, turning her in his arms, kissing her. He would always think of that first kiss, the warm lushness of her mouth, the taste of her on his tongue, her scent mingling with that of the Pacific breeze. "My surfer girl," he'd called her. He'd sworn that night that he was going to marry this woman or die trying.

10:46 a.m.

"WHAT?" Anna whispered as the ambulance turned a corner. Flint's expression had softened, his gaze almost dreamy, a slight smile on his lips. "Flint?"

He blinked, some of the softness going out of his face, his eyes. She regretted saying anything. For a few moments he'd been the Flint she'd fallen in love with.

"I was just thinking about the first time we kissed," he said quietly.

He couldn't have surprised her more. She shook her head, dragging her gaze away, not wanting him to see the impact his words had on her. How many times over the past five years had she relived that first date on the beach, her body achingly recalling the feel of being in his arms, the sensation of his lips on hers, the effect just one kiss had had on her?

But it was the last thing she wanted to think about now.

After that kiss, all her reservations about dating him had seemed to have gone out with the tide. When they'd walked back up the beach, holding hands, the surf ebbing around their bare feet, she'd known she would see him again if he asked.

He'd asked.

And she'd said yes, the taste of him still on her lips, the feel of him still humming through her veins. It was that kiss, their first kiss, that had convinced her. Flint Mauro had made one thing perfectly clear with all his actions—especially the kiss. He wanted her. She'd never been able to resist a man who knew what he wanted and went after it. She'd thought they'd had that in common.

"That night I thought nothing could keep us apart," he said now.

"So did I," she told him as the siren came on and the ambulance sped toward city hall. She could smell his light aftershave in the small enclosed space. It brought back the feel of his rough jaw, the whisper of his lips at her temple, then on her mouth. How could she have left this man?

"Anna." He leaned closer, his lips just inches from her own, his fingers brushing her cheek, warm, a feather of a touch that sent a shock wave through her.

The ambulance braked to a stop in front of city hall. "Anna, let me go in alone," Flint said. "It's not too late to stop this."

She pulled back from him, remembering now why she'd been forced to leave him. But for just an instant there, she'd almost kissed him, almost thought things could change between them, thought there was hope for them.

Shaking her head at her own foolishness, she popped open the back door and jumped down to the ground, turning to look back inside at him. "Just do your job, Flint."

His gaze turned hard again and she realized that was what she needed. She needed him to be the man who did whatever it took, just like his T-shirt had said. She didn't want to think of him as flesh and blood. She didn't want to remember their past.

She reached for one of the medical bags. "Once we're inside, remember, you're the doctor and I'm the nurse," she said. "Don't try to protect me."

FLINT NODDED ABRUPTLY, the moment lost. Just for an instant there, he'd thought he had seen that old devil desire in her eyes, he'd thought there was still a connection between them, he'd thought he could change her mind about this suicidal mission into hell. It was one thing for him to go in there. Another for her.

He climbed out. The brace hurt his leg. Limping wasn't a problem. He grabbed the oxygen tank and the other bag of medical supplies. They didn't look at each other as they started up the sidewalk.

He could feel eyes on them from inside the building but didn't look up. He stopped just in front of the door to put down the oxygen tanks and equipment as if they were too heavy for him.

Anna turned at the sound of his grunt. "Aren't you taking this a little too far?"

"I don't think so. I'm trying to act weak and helpless. How am I doing?"

She met his gaze and quickly looked away. "Good." Moving to the door, she waited until he joined her, then knocked. Her back was ramrod-straight, her expression unreadable. She could have been waiting for a bus.

This woman knew no fear, he told himself. That's why she was so calm. Fear, he'd always thought, was a good thing. It had saved his life more times than he wanted to count.

He looked over at Anna again, wondering if he'd ever really known her, as he waited for the SWAT team inside the building to open the door, waited to enter what might be the last door they ever walked through. Worst of all, he was walking through it with the only woman he'd ever loved.

THE PANIC CAME OUT of nowhere and with such acuteness that it took Anna's breath away. She'd done this hundreds of time, gone into situations that she'd known could get her killed, and yet she'd always been calm, trusting in her training. She'd thrived on this, pitting herself against whatever was behind the door she was just about to enter. She'd loved the challenge, loved the exhilaration, loved that her training could save lives, her own included.

But as she stood at the back door to city hall with Flint beside her, the panic took hold of her and she realized this time was different. This time she would be going in with a man she had loved, had planned to marry, a man who could have been the father to her children. This time the stakes were higher. This time she wasn't sure she could do this.

She felt herself begin to shake all over. This had never happened before. The SWAT team in Washington, D.C., used to make fun of her because she was so serene in some pretty hairy situations. Where was that unshakable cool now?

She glanced over at Flint. This was all his fault. He'd had to remind her of their first date, their first kiss. He'd had to remind her of what they'd shared all those years ago and thus remind her of all they had lost. Worse, he'd reminded her how much it had meant to her. Flint had been her first love. Her only love.

She hadn't let any man close since her breakup with Flint. Instead she'd gone back to being afraid of making the wrong decision when it came to men. With Flint, she had been so sure. And if he wasn't the right one, would she pick a man who was even more wrong for her next time? At the back of her mind was always the nagging fear that she would make the same mistake her older sister had made.

So she hadn't dated out of fear. And maybe something else. Maybe she hadn't dated because she still loved Flint.

Standing here, waiting for the door to city hall to open, she was forced to acknowledge there could be some truth to that. She still felt something for Flint. Something more than she had wanted to admit even to herself. And that changed everything. Suddenly she didn't want to go into this building. Not with Flint. She couldn't stand the thought that something might happen to him and she might not have the skills to save him.

And just as suddenly, she understood why he hated her doing this so much.

He looked over at her, his dark eyes hard as stones, and she felt a little calmer at the sight of his anger. But then his gaze softened, as if he could see what she was going through.

She looked away. She could do this. She had to. It didn't matter that Flint would be here with her. She would do what she'd always done—try to get everyone out of this alive.

But even as she thought it, she knew it *did* matter. This was Flint, and after all the years of denial about her feelings for him, suddenly she was scared.

CHAPTER SEVEN

11:01 a.m.

THE BACK DOOR of city hall was opened by one of the SWAT team, who quickly escorted Anna and Flint into the building. A half dozen men had all the doors in city hall secured on the first and third floors and were waiting for orders to storm the second floor again.

"You have your orders for audio and visual?" Flint asked the SWAT team member.

He nodded. "Standing by for audio and visual on your entrance." He glanced at Anna. Flint could see that the man was surprised she was going in, as well.

The attempt to take second floor had ended in a stalemate with the hostage takers holding a gun to Judge Craven's head. Flint had hated like hell to call them off. But had it escalated, Lee Harper might have blown up everyone, including the SWAT team members in the immediate area, not to mention Judge Craven.

Now the two subjects had half a dozen hostages as well as the judge. And in a few minutes, they could add Flint and Anna to their collection.

Flint could feel his heart pounding as they moved deeper into the old building. Their footsteps echoed on the marble floor, the sound eerie in the silent space. Anna looked cool as a cucumber, professional, capable and certainly not scared. But back at the door for a moment, he'd thought he'd seen vulnerability. He even thought he'd glimpsed fear.

He knew now that he must have been mistaken. Just as he'd been mistaken in the ambulance when he thought she wanted to kiss him as much as he'd wanted to kiss her. Yeah, for a moment he'd thought he had seen something of the woman he'd fallen in love with years ago. His mistake.

As they started up the wide central staircase to the second floor, Flint couldn't help himself. "Good luck," he whispered. "Whatever happens—"

"You, too," she said quickly without looking at him, and jogged up the stairs several ahead of him, as if afraid of what else he had been about to say.

11:04 a.m.

ANNA COULD HEAR someone yelling over the sound of crying as she and Flint reached the second floor. Glancing down the hall, she saw the splintered wood on the floor outside the meeting room where the lock had busted. The door had a hole the size of a fist in it. What looked like a desk had been shoved against the door, blocking a view into the meeting room.

She knew there were SWAT team members positioned close by, but she didn't see a soul.

"You need a doctor in there?" Flint called as they neared the end of the hallway.

The crying halted. So did the yelling. "Get the door open," Anna heard Kenny order, recognizing his voice. "Check to make sure it isn't a trick, then search them."

A moment later she heard scraping sounds as several large items were moved away from the door. Then the desk was slid aside and a face appeared. An older man, his hair gray, face lined, eyes wide, blank behind the wire-rimmed glasses. Lee Harper.

The door groaned open and Anna got her first glimpse of the situation. Her heart began to pound wildly. No matter how many times she witnessed a scene like this, she could never stand the terror she saw in the victims's faces.

Lee Harper, slightly hunched over, stepped in front of her, blocking her view. He wore a police uniform and a large police-issue coat. The coat was open and she could see what appeared to be a homemade bomb duct-taped to his chest. A digital watch was attached to a 9-volt battery and a blasting cap was stuck into a block of green plastic. In an indentation in the explosives was a red toggle switch. Lee held his finger against the switch as he stepped toward them.

Out of the corner of her eye Anna could see Flint studying the bomb with an experienced eye. If there was any chance the bomb was a fake… She waited, knowing that Flint would have made his move by now if that were the case.

"Search them and their bags, but make it quick," Kenny ordered. "I'm friggin' bleeding to death in here."

Anna dropped her bag and stepped back as Lee motioned her to do. He bent down, keeping an eye on them both as he dug through the bag with his free hand, then shoved the bag behind him.

She watched him search Flint's medical bag, noticing the way Lee kept his finger on the switch. It was a real bomb. She saw Flint's grim expression and felt her breath catch in her throat.

Lee did a cursory search of her body, asking her politely to unzip her bulletproof vest, then checking each of the pockets along the legs of her pants before he did the same with Flint.

Anna could sense that Flint wanted to stop this now, before it got any worse. But Lee kept his fingers on the switch. Any movement and the bomb would be detonated. Flint must have seen that in the man's eyes. Anna had. Kenny might be the loud, volatile one, but Lee was the truly dangerous one. Especially after everything she'd learned about him before coming up here.

Past him, Anna studied the hostages. They were all handcuffed to the old radiators along the wall under the large windows. The blinds were drawn, but in the glow of the fluorescent lights overhead, their eyes shone with hope at just the sight of her and Flint. Five men. One woman. Where was Lorna Sinke?

"Help us!" the woman in the corner cried. Councilwoman Gwendolyn Clark.

Anna didn't recognize any of the others, but she could only assume the impeccable man in the dark suit near the councilwoman was her uncle, Judge Lawrence Craven. He appeared to be trying to comfort and quiet her, without much luck.

From where she stood, Anna couldn't see Kenny or

Lorna Sinke. She just prayed the woman was still alive and that she could get her to the hospital before it was too late. She and Flint had a lot of people's lives in their hands. She couldn't imagine leaving this room without all of the hostages.

As Lee finished searching them, he seemed to see Flint for the first time. His expression made it clear that he was having second thoughts about letting him into the room. Lee seemed to sense it would be a mistake.

Anna held her breath, afraid what Flint would do if Lee insisted she go in alone.

"Get them in here and barricade the door," Kenny yelled from inside the room.

Anna shifted a little to one side and spotted Kenny. He was on the right side of the room. He hadn't seen Flint yet because he was sprawled on the floor, his back against the wall, his feet splayed. He was yelling obscenities and clutching his upper arm, his fingers dark with blood.

Still, Lee hesitated.

"You have an injured man in there?" Flint demanded.

"Let the doctor in," Kenny called. "What the hell is taking you so long? I'm in here friggin' bleeding."

With obvious reservations, Lee motioned them in, barricading the door behind them. Flint took another look at the bomb as he passed Lee, and they all entered the room.

Kenny balanced the assault rifle on one leg, his fingers on the trigger. Lee still had a finger on the bomb switch. The air almost cracked as if the atoms were charged. Anything could happen in this room.

To make matters worse, Anna saw that several of the

hostages knew Flint was a police officer—including Gwendolyn Clark. Her eyes widened in surprise as she recognized him. Did she know he was the head of the SWAT team? Surely she wouldn't be fool enough to say anything. The judge whispered something to his niece that seemed to warn her, as if he, too, feared she would blow Flint's cover.

As Anna stepped deeper into the room, she saw the woman lying on the floor, away from the others, and quickly moved to her.

Lorna Sinke was in her late forties, slim to the point of severity. She wore a pretty blue dress, the front soaked with blood, and held a wadded-up suit jacket to her chest. Anna noted that one of the male hostages wasn't wearing a suit jacket and had blood all over his shirt and hands, but he didn't look injured.

Anna knelt beside Lorna.

"Don't worry about that stupid bitch," Kenny yelled at Anna. "Can't you see I'm bleeding over here?"

As per plan, Flint put down the oxygen tank and, taking his medical jump kit, headed for Kenny, his limp even more pronounced as he moved across the floor.

"We don't need her yet," Anna heard Flint say. "Just try to relax. Let's see how badly you've been hurt."

"It hurts like hell, Doc," Kenny whined. "One of those bastards shot me."

Across the room, Anna leaned close to her patient. "I'm Anna Carson," she said quietly as she opened her bag and pulled on a pair of latex gloves.

"Lorna Sinke," the woman said in a surprisingly strong voice.

"How are you doing?" Anna asked, surveying the situation.

"Not bad considering I've been shot in the chest," Lorna said. It appeared the woman had been shot on the right side. The bleeding had been controlled with direct pressure. She appeared to be experiencing some minor difficulty breathing.

Anna pulled out bandages, blood pressure cuff, stethoscope, trauma dressings.

"I'm going to need something to cover her with," she said, turning to Lee. She could hear Flint behind her, trying to calm Kenny down.

The tension in the room was so thick the air felt too heavy to breathe. Gwendolyn Clark was still sniveling in the corner, but other than that the room had gone silent. Anna wondered if the techs had been able to get the audio and visual in. She didn't dare look up to check.

"Tell me what happened," she said to Lorna. "Do you know what you were shot with?"

"Happened too fast."

"Try to remain still." Anna asked her about her medical history. Was she allergic to any drugs? Was she taking anything?

"We have audio and visual," Max said softly into her earpiece.

She nodded and smiled down at Lorna. "We're doing fine here," she said, taking the woman's free hand. "Don't you worry. Everything's going to be fine."

Lorna gave her a get-real look, as if no one could be that naive.

As FLINT OPENED the medical bag and took out a pair of latex gloves, he could feel Kenny's gaze on him. He worked methodically, taking his time, trying to appear more put out than anything else. A doctor coming in here would be scared spitless, but he knew that emergency-room doctors saw stuff on a daily basis that would curl Flint's hair.

"You a doctor here in town?" Kenny asked.

"Please try to remain still," Flint said impatiently. He could feel the man's eyes on him, sense the growing concern. He kept his face expressionless as he picked up the trauma scissors and, gently removing Kenny's fingers from the upper arm, carefully began to cut away the fabric of the uniform shirt from the area around the gunshot.

"You don't look like a doctor," Kenny said, his voice sounding too high.

"What does a doctor look like?" Flint asked, trying to sound bored.

Kenny had the assault rifle next to him, his hand on it. But he and Flint both knew he would have a hell of a time trying to shoot anyone with it one-handed. And there was no way he could get it up and pointed at Flint. They were too close. Taking the rifle away from Kenny would have been as easy as taking candy from a baby.

But Kenny wasn't the immediate problem. Flint had seen the look in Lee's eyes. He could feel the older man's gaze boring into his back even now. As Lorna had told them, Lee was the smart one. He was also the loose cannon. Flint had seen something in the old man's eyes that had frozen his blood solid. Lee *wanted* to flip that switch. He wanted to end this and was fighting like hell not to.

Flint knew he could take Kenny right now without any trouble. But he needed a better look at that bomb. It had a timer, but that could be set to go off just seconds after the switch was flipped—not minutes. Flint couldn't risk it. Not yet. He would have to wait and see if he could get a few of the hostages out first.

He just had to be careful. If he did anything suspicious, he knew it would push Lee to detonate the bomb and take them all with him.

"What did you do to your leg?" Kenny asked, sounding as if he was in pain, but also nervous.

"Motorcycle crash," Flint said. "I used to like to race bikes."

"No kidding? I didn't know doctors did things like that."

"This is going to sting," Flint warned as he started to swab the area with disinfectant.

"Sting?" Kenny cursed.

Flint gave him a don't-be-such-a-big-baby look.

Kenny calmed down a little, grimacing each time Flint touched his shoulder.

"I have to see how bad the injury is," Flint said as he cleaned around the bullet hole. He didn't want to tell Kenny that the lead had passed right through the fleshy part of his arm. Just a flesh wound. He would live. Unlike Lorna Sinke, unless they could get her to the hospital.

Flint could hear Anna talking softly to Lorna; he could hear the worry in her tone.

"What were you shot with?" he asked Kenny, following Anna's lead.

"A gun."

"What caliber?" Flint asked.

"How the hell would I know? The asshole shot me and then must have thrown the gun out the window." He glared at the hostages.

"Well, you were lucky. The bullet passed right through the fleshy part of your arm and missed the bone."

"I don't feel lucky," Kenny groused. "It hurts like hell."

Imagine what being shot in the chest feels like in comparison, Flint wanted to say. Instead he took his time as he cleaned the wound. He could hear Anna on the other side of the room, working on Lorna, but he didn't dare show an interest. Kenny had made it clear he would just as soon let the council aide die.

Nor did Flint look behind him at Lee. He doubted it would take much of anything to get Lee to detonate that bomb. Flint didn't want to add to the man's suspicions, but he also needed a closer look at the bomb. He'd seen that type of mechanism before and knew he could render it safe if he could get his hands on it before that switch was flipped. Little chance of that.

The timer was the dead giveaway. There were certain things a bomb needed to be triggered. A spark was required to set off the plastic explosives. A blasting cap would do the trick.

And there was only one reason to put a timer on a bomb. To have a delay before the explosion. The delay could be anywhere from seconds to hours.

Flint just hoped the delay would be long enough.

11:54 a.m.

ANNA TURNED TO Lee and saw that he was watching Flint like a hawk. She'd seen his suspicion and knew she had to avert it away from Flint.

"I need something to cover her up with," she said. "Lee?"

He turned, surprised she knew his name.

Anna held her breath. She could see him trying to remember if Kenny had said his name in front of her. Otherwise, how would the nurse know his name?

"I need something to cover her, to keep her warm," Anna repeated.

Lee glanced around. This was Southern California. No one wore coats this time of year. No one but Lee Harper. "I don't know—"

"Could she use your police coat?" Anna asked.

Across the room, Anna could almost feel Flint hold his breath. If she could get Lee's coat off, Flint would have a better look at the bomb and its workings.

Lee looked down at Lorna, then nodded slowly. "I didn't mean to shoot her." He shrugged out of the coat, still keeping one hand close to the switch in case this was some sort of trick. Clearly he felt guilty for shooting Lorna and didn't want to see her die.

Across the room, Flint seemed to relax a little as he applied one of the four-by-four trauma dressings to Kenny's arm. "You really need to get a shot of antibiotics so this doesn't get infected. You could lose your arm if that happens. I'd suggest you get to a hospital as soon as possible."

"Yeah, I'll do that as soon as I get out of the country, Doc."

"How is she?" Lee asked Anna quietly.

"She needs to get to a hospital."

"She isn't going anywhere," Kenny snapped, overhearing them. "Are you about done, Doc?"

"Just about."

"I know you don't want her to die," Anna said quietly to Lee.

"Speak for yourself," Kenny snapped. "It's her fault I'm shot."

"She didn't shoot you," Lee said.

"Oh, yeah, then who did? Huh?" Kenny demanded. "One of them did. I wouldn't be surprised if that bitch has a gun hidden under her dress and is just waiting to shoot *you*."

"I'm wearing a bomb," Lee said, his voice deadly calm. "No one is stupid enough to shoot me."

Kenny looked at Lee as if he wouldn't put money on that. "Ouch. Can you be any rougher?" he demanded of Flint.

"Sorry. I just need to make sure I get the wound properly dressed so you don't get gangrene." That shut Kenny up. Temporarily.

Anna feared what Kenny would do once his arm was bandaged. She covered her patient, then attached the blood pressure cuff, pumped it up and listened. Lorna's blood pressure was only slightly elevated, which was surprising, considering what she'd been through.

Anna listened to her lungs. The bullet had missed her heart. Her breathing was a little shallow, making Anna suspect one of her lungs might have been hit. She listened more closely. There were breath sounds on both sides, but none in the lower lobes. A lung had probably been nicked on the lower edge, she suspected.

As she started to put the oxygen mask over Lorna's mouth and nose, Lorna stopped her and drew her close.

Anna bent down, pretending to listen to Lorna's chest.

"There are cookies in my bag," Lorna whispered, her fingers digging into Anna's arm. "They're drugged."

Anna froze, pulling back a little to look into the woman's eyes. Lorna was as tense as a wire strung too tightly, but Anna suspected that had nothing to do with her pain or her fear. In fact, Lorna had been eerily calm through all of this.

Drugged? Anna mouthed the word so only Lorna could see.

Lorna nodded.

Why in the world would the council aide bring "drugged" cookies to work? Anna remembered the special meeting of the council and attorneys, seemingly to discuss getting rid of Lorna Sinke. Had Lorna known about the meeting? Had she been bringing the cookies for the council?

"What drug?" Anna mouthed.

"Xenaline."

Anna raised a brow. Xenaline had the same effect as alcohol on the system. It would give the appearance of being drunk, slurred speech, staggering, an inability to think straight, loss of muscular function, depending on how much was administered. "How much?"

"One, mellow. Three, drunk. Four, a stupor. Six, pushing up daisies," Lorna said matter-of-factly.

Anna thought about the alleged murder of Lorna's elderly parents. Who was this woman? Was this frail little thing capable of murdering her own parents?

Well, this frail little thing had a container full of drugged cookies. Obviously, Lorna Sinke seemed to be quite capable of just about anything. She was the one who'd gotten away from Lee and Kenny. She was the one who had been running the show in this room. And she was still going strong after being shot in the chest.

Anna looked down at the woman with a kind of awe mixed with horror. As sole caregiver to her elderly parents, Lorna had had opportunity, as well as motive. What were the chances that both parents had fallen down the basement stairs and broken their necks? Almost nil.

Anna wished now that she had asked what drug had been found in Lorna's car and ruled inadmissible.

She had a pretty good idea, though. A drug that could make an elderly couple disoriented enough to fall down a flight of basement stairs.

As she looked down at Lorna Sinke, Anna tried to figure out how she could use the cookies without making the hostage takers suspicious. She met Lorna's gaze. "Don't worry, I'll think of something."

Lorna nodded and closed her eyes, a smile on her lips. "Make sure Gwendolyn gets the lion's share."

CHAPTER EIGHT

12:39 p.m.

ANNA LOOKED to the other side of the room. Flint's broad back was bent over Kenny. If she could have reached him, she would have laid her hand on his back. She knew it would have felt strong and warm, as if the memory were from yesterday—not five years ago.

She took a breath, her heart pounding faster. After that first date, Flint had asked her out again. How would she like to have Chinese food at this place he'd heard about?

"I love Chinese food," she'd said in surprise.

"Good. I'd love to have dinner with you tomorrow night."

"Tomorrow night?"

"Too soon, huh?"

The oops sound in his voice had made her laugh. "No, tomorrow would be fine." She'd realized that she wanted to see him again as badly as he did her.

He'd taken her to what turned out to be her favorite Chinese food place near the beach. Then he'd ordered potstickers with the spicy dipping sauce only this particular Chinese restaurant offered—her favorite.

When she commented on it, he confessed. "I called

and asked your mother about your favorite restaurant and what to order."

"You *called* my mother?" She didn't mean to sound so surprised that he'd phoned her mother. In fact, she was even more surprised that her mother had known the answer.

"Actually, she put your dad on the phone. He told me you loved this place because of their potstickers."

"How did you find my parents' phone number?"

He grinned. "Do you have any idea how many Carsons there are in the phone book in this area?"

"What if my parents hadn't lived around here?" she asked, amazed that he'd gone to that much trouble—and a little concerned. All this after only one date?

"I might have had to put off dinner for a few weeks or possibly years," he joked.

She shook her head at him. "Or you could have just asked me what I like to eat."

He nodded. "That was an option, but I wanted to surprise you."

He had, in more ways than one.

They'd had a wonderful meal, then walked along the beach, the lights of the city glittering over the bay.

She'd had her reservations about him, but by the end of the night, she found herself hoping that he would kiss her again. He didn't disappoint her.

Their first kiss had been all fireworks. This one was gentle, just like his arms around her. Flint Mauro was a man of many talents. He just kept amazing her. And he clearly wanted her.

But he wasn't going to push her. He must have sensed

the hesitancy in her. He just didn't know why she needed to take it slow, why dating scared her, why getting close to a man terrified her....

Anna listened to Lorna's heart. Strong. She smiled down at the woman. She couldn't help admiring her, the way she'd handled herself through all of this. Lorna looked like anything but a killer. If it wasn't for the drugged cookies, Anna might have convinced herself Lorna had been unjustly accused in her parents' deaths.

No matter, it wasn't Anna's place to judge this woman. But Anna suspected that if anyone could survive this ordeal, it would be Lorna Sinke.

Sitting back, Anna studied the woman. She wondered about the relationship Lorna must have had with *her* mother. Anna couldn't help but think about her own mother and their so-called relationship. Her mother had called the day after Anna had gone out with Flint and invited her to Sunday dinner.

Anna had thought it strange at the time, since she hadn't heard from her mother in months, even though they lived in the same city. Anna saw her dad every week; they had a standing lunch date on Thursdays.

Curious, she'd accepted the invitation.

"Who is this Flint Mauro who called us the other day?" her mother demanded the moment Anna arrived at the house that Sunday. Her sister Emily and husband Lance were there, as well.

Her parents had lived in an upper-middle-class neighborhood in Courage Bay. Her father was an accountant with a large local firm and her mother had always been a stay-at-home mom.

Anna and her mother had never been close. Anna had been the tomboy, all skinned knees and frogs in her pockets. Her mother had related better to Anna's sisters. Candace had been six years older than Anna, and Anna felt as though she'd never known her older sister, who was only interested in dating, makeup and hanging out in her room with her friends when she was a teenager.

Emily, who was three years younger than Anna, played with dolls, loved pretty frilly dresses and took ballet lessons. Anna, who played Little League, hated dresses and had more in common with the boys in the neighborhood, felt like the black sheep of the family.

Only her father seemed to accept her and appreciate her athletic abilities. He'd given her a baseball glove for her sixth birthday. Her mother had had a fit and the two had fought about it.

Anna hadn't wanted to talk to her mother about Flint. She hadn't even mentioned him to her father. It was too soon and she feared talking about him might jinx things.

"He asked all kinds of questions about you," her mother said.

"He just wanted to know what kind of food you liked," her dad amended from his recliner. He smiled at Anna over the magazine he'd been reading. He was a tall, handsome man with brown eyes and hair, and a kind face.

"How well do you know this young man?" her mother demanded. When Anna thought of her mother, she thought of how bony and hard the woman had always felt when she'd hugged her. There was nothing soft there, nothing loving or generous, as if her spare body was an indication of what was inside.

"We've been out twice. He has four brothers, he grew up in Michigan, he's a cop." Anna was gratified to see her mother's horrified expression.

"He sounds quite nice," her father said.

"You think everyone is nice," was her mother's comment. "What do you know about his family? Mauro. I don't think I know that name." She looked toward Emily's husband Lance, the former football star now car salesman at his father's dealership.

"He's only been in town two weeks," Anna said quickly, knowing that Lance would make a point of checking up on Flint. Lance did whatever her sister wanted him to do, and Emily did whatever their mother wanted her to do.

It had been their mother's idea that Lance and Emily wait a minimum of four years after their wedding to have children. "That way, you know the marriage is going to work before you involve children," their mother had said.

As if four years were a magic number. Clearly, all Emily was prepared for in life was being someone's wife and the mother of his children. She had picked out her china when she was thirteen.

Anna had wanted more than that. More than what her mother had wanted. And she'd felt guilty because of it, as if her wanting more diminished what Emily and her mother had. As if they felt the same way.

"You'll have to bring your young man by sometime," her father said when he walked Anna to her car after dinner.

She'd dodged her mother's and Emily's pointed

questions about Flint all evening. "I'll give that some thought," she said, telling herself there was no way she would ever subject Flint to her family. "Anyway, I'm not sure he'll call again."

There was a twinkle in her father's eye. "Oh, you'll be seeing him again."

Of course, her father had been right, Anna thought, looking over at Flint. Except neither of them could have predicted how badly it would turn out.

12:58 p.m.

KENNY WATCHED LEE, his irritation with the guy growing. What had he been thinking, hooking up with a guy who was so crazy he'd tape a bomb to his chest? I mean, the guy could flip that switch and blow them all to kingdom come just for the hell of it. If anything, Lee looked more unhinged today than when Kenny first met him.

Kenny had planned to shoot him and put him out of his misery by now, and he would have, if it hadn't been for the damned bomb.

He narrowed his gaze. Had Lee figured that out somehow? Was that why he hadn't just brought a gun like a normal person?

Licking his lips, Kenny told himself he needed to be cooler with Lee. Not a good idea to push the fool over the edge. Better to try to pacify him. What would it hurt?

Once he got his money and was on that plane, Kenny couldn't care less what Lee did. But in the meantime....

"I should put in that call for you," he said. Lee didn't seem to hear him. "Lee?" The old man looked up as if surprised to still find himself here. "I promised you air time on television. I'll tell the cops and get on that. Get you on the evening news. Should be easier than money and a plane, huh. As soon as the doctor gets me patched up, I'll make that call."

He hadn't expected the old guy to dance a jig, but a little enthusiasm would have been nice.

Instead, Lee just looked at him, barely nodding in acknowledgment, making Kenny wish he hadn't bothered.

IT WAS A BAD DREAM. Lee told himself he would wake up any minute, wake up to Francine shaking his shoulder. "You were snoring again," she would say, then smile. "Roll over, honey." And he would, and she would cuddle next to him, slipping her arm around his waist, and he would fall back to sleep.

He closed his eyes for a moment, his finger trembling a little against the bomb switch.

Just do it. End it, he said silently. What are you waiting for? You don't want to be here. You sure don't want to go on television and talk about Francine. Had that been his idea?

He couldn't remember. He couldn't remember anything since Francine had died. No, he thought, it had started before that. He remembered Francine covering for him at a faculty party. The man she'd married, the one who used to be able to recite poetry for hours to his English classes, now couldn't remember the most basic poem.

When he opened his eyes he wished he *had* been dreaming. But he was awake. This was real. His gaze fell on Kenny. Oh, indeed this was happening, and only he could stop it before it was too late.

Too late for what? he wondered. He glanced at the woman on the floor, trying to remember what exactly it was that had reminded him of Francine.

"Are you all right? Lee?"

He dragged himself up out of wherever it was he spent most of his days now. Limbo.

"Are you all right? You need to sit down?" Kenny was calling to him.

He shook his head. "Fine."

Kenny didn't look convinced. Lee felt beads of sweat break out across his forehead. He felt clammy and cold one minute, burning up the next, as if the fire was in his head.

Kenny was still staring at him, looking concerned and at the same time keeping his distance, as if by staying across the room, he would be safe when the bomb went off. Obviously, Kenny knew nothing about bombs.

THE TENSION IN THE ROOM seemed to jump several degrees. Anna turned again to look at Flint's broad back. She watched him put a bandage on Kenny's arm. With his large hands, he was having trouble getting the bandage on straight. She stared at his hands. It was impossible not to remember the feel of his fingers on her skin.

The first time they'd made love had been at the beach. Anna felt a familiar ache at the memory. She could imagine the sun on her skin, the soft warm feel of the sand beneath her. They'd spent the afternoon swimming and walking the beach, talking. As the sun slid into the Pacific, they'd stopped at an outcropping of rocks south of town. His kiss had been pure heat. It burned through her to her core. His fingers had felt cool against her skin as he'd brushed glistening sand crystals from her shoulder, his gaze meeting hers.

Yes. Yes. Yes. She'd wanted him as she had never wanted anything before. She'd felt a wild abandon. Giving herself to Flint was impossible—even the thought of surrendering to him frightened her—and making love would have been the ultimate surrender.

The beach had been empty, the day quickly giving way to night. She'd felt the sea breeze coming off the water, warm against her skin as he'd slipped one strap of her swimsuit down over her shoulder, then the other, revealing the pale skin of her breasts beneath.

Flint had let out the smallest of aahs, his gaze skimming over her bare skin like warm fingers. Then he'd met her gaze and kissed her.

She realized he was looking at her now. His gaze seemed to soften at the sight of her, as if he'd known what she'd been thinking about. She felt herself blush and glanced away for a moment, not wanting him to see how much she still ached for his touch.

"Nurse, could you help me with this?" Flint asked softly.

Anna sensed Kenny's gaze on her as she crossed the room. The look in his eyes told her everything she needed to know. If his demands weren't met, he wouldn't hesitate to take it out on everyone within sight.

But it was Lee, the older man, she was still worried most about. He looked exhausted, and yet so nervous he was almost at the point of pacing. He needed the situation resolved, and soon. This was a man who had been pushed into a corner and would do anything to get out. In his emotional state, Anna knew he could detonate the bomb. For any reason.

Or just forget and flip the switch, as if he no longer understood what would happen when he did. Max had gotten all the information he could on Lee Harper. A respected, loved English professor at the local college, he had retired a year ago after he'd been diagnosed with Alzheimer's.

The loss of his wife had only added to his stress, which in turn had sped the disease. Lee couldn't be trusted not to flip the bomb switch at any time.

Anna moved in beside Flint and began to help him with the bandage. Kenny watched her for a moment, then settled his gaze on Flint.

"You have arthritis in your hands," Anna said to Flint.

He looked up at her in surprise, but caught on quickly to what she was doing. "I don't think that is any of your business, nurse."

"Sorry." She turned back to Kenny and felt him relax a little, thinking the doc had a reason for not being good with bandages.

The moment she'd secured the bandage to Kenny's arm, he ordered both Flint and her back. They moved across the room from him, over by Lorna.

Anna checked her patient. Lorna was awake and having a little more trouble breathing, but definitely alert.

Anna looked past Lorna to Flint. "If we can take Kenny out, I think we might be able to reason with Lee," she whispered to him.

Flint gave her a look as if to say he wasn't so sure about that. "Let's get Lorna out of here first."

Lorna mumbled something under the oxygen mask. Anna moved it a little so she could hear her.

"Get the bastards," Lorna whispered. "Don't worry about me."

Anna smiled down at the woman and put the oxygen mask back. "You just take it easy, okay?"

Lorna's eyes glinted and she nodded.

"If everything goes to hell, you take Kenny," Flint said. "I'll take care of Lee and the bomb."

Anna nodded, not wanting to think about Flint that close to the bomb should it go off. She'd had a little experience with bombs in Washington, D.C. She knew Lee wasn't wearing enough explosives to level city hall. That would take a truckload. But there was enough to take out this room—and possibly the outer wall.

"What are you doing?" Kenny demanded, swinging the rifle toward them. "Stop whispering."

He grimaced and looked at his arm. He was in obvious pain, but that wasn't what had him so strung out.

"You got something in that bag for the pain?" Kenny asked her. "Some Percodan or OxyContin."

"The police wouldn't allow us to bring in any of those kinds of drugs," she said.

Kenny swore and came over to grab her medical bag. He dug through it. "You've got to have something. What's this?"

"It's a drug for congestive heart failure. It would definitely calm you and might relieve your anxiety, but it probably wouldn't help much for the pain."

"What kind of pills do you have?"

She shook her head. "Everything we have, cardiac drugs and drugs for narcotic overdoses, have to be administered through an IV or IM."

"IM?"

"Intramuscular." She'd seen how jittery he'd become and recognized the symptoms. "The doctor could call and get something prescribed for you."

Kenny looked at Flint, hope in his eyes. "You could get me some Percodan? Enough to last me for a while?"

"It's a very addictive prescription drug," Flint said, and frowned.

"No shit, Doc. My sister used to get it for me, but you bastards killed her."

"Your sister was a doctor?" Flint asked.

"Nah," he said with a laugh. "She was a products manager for a company that tested car engines. But she got me some drugs sometimes." Kenny looked as if he wished he hadn't said anything. "She knew I needed them or she wouldn't have got them. My sister was a good kid. She took care of me. Loaned me money and did nice stuff like that."

"What happened to your sister?" Anna asked, not wanting to think how she'd obtained the drugs.

"She was killed in a basement fire after the quake," Kenny said, an edge to his voice. "The fire department didn't get to her in time. She was trapped inside. This city killed her just as sure as it killed Lee's wife. His old lady was crushed when the convenience store where she worked fell on her."

"So that's what this is about," Judge Craven said

from across the room. "You blame the city for the aftershock of an earthquake, a natural disaster?"

Kenny shot him a withering look. "Where was the city when my sister was burning to death, or when Lee's wife was lying under that store roof? Anyway, I told all of you to keep your mouths shut. Especially that dumb broad."

"I am not a dumb broad," Gwendolyn snapped. "I happen to be a respected member of this community, and I'm sick of watching you all cater to these...criminals." The last she directed at Flint and Anna.

Anna gave her a pleading look to shut up. Gwendolyn returned it with a dirty look.

"I can understand how you must feel," Anna said quickly, turning back to Kenny, who was glaring at Gwendolyn. Anna pretended to tuck a piece of his bandage in, trying to draw his attention away from the councilwoman. "That must have been a terrible loss for you."

"Yeah. Lee wants an apology from the mayor on the television news," Kenny said. "I want a hell of a lot more than an apology. The city owes me big-time and it's going to pay."

Anna glanced at Flint. That was the connection between the two men. Death. And someone to blame. Kenny blamed the city for his sister's death. She had also been his source of pills. Probably his source of income, as well. Kenny wanted someone to pay. Lee, she thought, just wanted his anguish to be felt, his voice to be heard. And if that bomb went off, it would be heard loud and clear, the repercussions felt for a long time to come.

"The city owes me." Kenny was looking at Anna as if he expected an argument out of her.

Not likely. She'd been trained to deal with hostage takers and knew that you played along, were always compliant, never argued. Everyone in the room seemed to understand how that worked except Gwendolyn Clark.

"I'm sorry to hear about your sister," Anna said. "I'm sure she was a nice woman."

"Yeah." Kenny looked around the room, as if trying to decide who to take his frustration out on.

The phone rang and Anna knew it was Max's doing. He was monitoring the room from the audio and video devices that she knew were peering out of the air vents, although she hadn't dared look up.

Kenny picked up the phone, seemingly irritated that he was interrupted. "Where the hell is my money and my plane?" he shrieked into the receiver.

Anna could hear Max's side of the conversation in her earpiece. "It takes a little time," Max said to Kenny. "While we're waiting, why don't we talk?"

"If you think you're going to talk me out of my demands—"

"I'm working on your demands. I also don't want you hurting anyone else while we're waiting. So, are you from Courage Bay?"

"I know how this works. I tell you my pathetic life story and you pretend to feel sorry for me, act like you care about me, and I start feeling bad and you talk me out of this." Kenny laughed. "Save it for some sucker."

"I'm sorry to hear about your sister, Kenny," Max said. "Patty Reese. The two of you were close?"

Kenny let out a groan. "Okay, so you know about my

sister. You also know that she died because the city didn't get to her soon enough to save her."

"A natural disaster like an earthquake definitely stretches the city's ability to help everyone," Max agreed.

"Don't give me that. The city is to blame," Kenny snapped. "You owe me. You let my sister burn to death."

Anna was surprised to see that Lee had moved over beside Kenny. He'd been so quiet, she hadn't heard him.

Kenny seemed surprised and a little upset to see Lee so close, as well. He stared at Lee for a moment, then said into the phone, "I need a video camera," as if it was an afterthought. No doubt it was. "We're going to make a statement to the press. You're going to make sure it's on the television news." He looked up at Lee, then nodded and said into the phone, "Leave the camera outside the door. No tricks."

"Can you give me something in return as a show of faith here, Kenny?" Max asked. "I got you the doctor and nurse. I need some hostages so I can say to my bosses, he's working with us here."

Kenny was already looking at the hostages. "Sure. You can have a councilman."

Obviously Kenny had changed his mind about releasing Gwendolyn Clark, Anna thought. But she knew Max's priority was to get Lorna out of the room and to the hospital.

"I was hoping for the injured woman, Kenny," Max said. "I just don't want her to die on us. That would definitely slow down your demands."

"Just get the video camera," Kenny insisted. "I'll

give you a councilman and then I'll send out the video cassette with the bitch."

"Along with the doctor and nurse," Max said.

"Sure." Kenny hung up.

Anna shot a look at Flint. Kenny was being too agreeable. This didn't feel right. She could see that Flint shared her concern.

Just minutes later Anna heard the tap at the door. Kenny removed the handcuffs from the councilman with the blood on his shirt. Anna saw the man give Lorna a reassuring smile as he let Kenny shove him toward the door, the barrel of the assault rifle pressed to the back of his head.

The councilman opened the door, Kenny staying behind him as he picked up the video camera. Once the councilman had the camera, Kenny backed him up slowly through the door into the room, grabbed the camera, shoved the councilman out and barricaded the door.

"One hostage out," Flint whispered. But he looked worried, Anna thought. Kenny was being too accommodating.

The room filled with a heavy silence as Kenny handed the camera to Lee. The older man set the camera on one of the shelves along the far wall. Still keeping that one finger on the bomb toggle, he turned the camera on with his other hand.

The camera began to roll. Lee stared into the lens, swallowed, then pulled a sheet of paper from his pocket and slowly read, his voice full of emotion, his words obviously carefully chosen.

"Francine Harper was my wife of forty-seven years. Her death devastated my life. She was everything to me. But she is only one of the souls lost during the aftershock that hit this area almost two months ago," he said, reading the sheet. "The city wasn't prepared, and because of that, lives were lost, families were destroyed. The city council talks about money and manpower. How much is a life worth? What if it was one of their loved ones trapped for hours under the roof of a convenience store? Wouldn't they find the money for manpower then?" He looked into the camera. "The city can no longer make excuses. Another earthquake here is inevitable. Steps must be taken to see that there is the manpower to save the lives of the people who depend on this city."

Tears welled in his eyes. He folded the paper awkwardly with one hand and put it back into his pocket and turned off the camera.

Kenny had been watching silently, contempt in his expression, but also a wariness. Like the rest of them, he wasn't sure what Lee would do now.

1:33 p.m.

KENNY LOOKED UP to find Lee standing over him, his finger stuck in that damned bomb. For a moment he almost told Lee what he could do with that bomb, but something in Lee's gaze—

"It's time we released more of the hostages," Lee said.

"Okay," Kenny agreed. What did he care? "You can have any of them you want. Except for the judge. He stays. No matter what."

Councilwoman Gwendolyn Clark heard the exchange and stopped sniveling, her eyes following Kenny, her face flushed with the thought of getting out of the room alive.

Lee nodded slowly and reached for the phone. "We will be sending out several hostages with the video camera. The tape is to run on the news."

"The earliest we can get on will be the five o'clock news," Max said.

"Five o'clock news?" Kenny snapped. "I'm not waiting around till five o'clock for some damned—"

"That will be fine," Lee said, and took the phone from Kenny's hand. "That will be fine." He hung up.

Kenny stared at him. Who the hell did this guy think he was? Lee was a total wacko. A wacko with a bomb, he reminded himself.

ANNA COULDN'T IMAGINE Kenny waiting around until five o'clock for his money, let alone the news. Not only that, Lee would have no way of knowing if his tape had made the news, since there was no TV in the meeting room.

Clearly the only way to get these people out of this room safely was through Lee.

"I'm sorry about your wife," Anna said quietly to the elderly man.

"Francine," Lee said on a breath that could have been a sob.

"That's a pretty name," she said. "You must have loved her very much."

He nodded, as if unable to speak, and met her gaze. "She was a good woman."

Anna wondered what his wife would have thought of this.

"I just had to do...something," he said, as if reading her mind. He looked ill. His face was pale and his eyes were fogged over with tears or grief or the disease that was eating away at his brain.

Kenny had picked up the phone once Lee moved back to his position near the door.

"Don't tell me what I agreed to," Kenny was yelling into the receiver. "I said I would give you a hostage. I did. Now I want something more from you. I want my damned money."

Anna could hear Max through her earpiece negotiating with Kenny. "It will make it easier to get the items you requested if Lorna Sinke doesn't die. It would definitely be a show of faith and help me get the people in charge of the city to speed things up."

Kenny actually seemed to consider this. He glared at Lorna with obvious animosity, then looked at Gwendolyn Clark. She had been listening to Kenny's end of the conversation, as well, and now started crying loudly, saying, "Please let me go. Please let me go."

"You can have a woman," Kenny snapped. "The councilwoman broad. I'm sick of listening to her."

Anna felt her heart drop. If only Gwendolyn would just shut up. Like Lorna, she wanted to strangle the woman.

Gwendolyn quit crying. She wiped her tears and looked more eager than ever to get away. She didn't seem to have any problem leaving her uncle, the judge, behind, or any of the rest of them.

"It would be easier to take the injured woman out now," Max said. "The medical personnel can bring her out with them. If she dies, there could be a problem getting you a passport."

"Listen—"

"I'm doing the best I can here, but I'm only the chief of police," Max told him. "I take my orders from the commissioner, and ultimately we're looking at the FBI getting involved. Their policy is not to negotiate at all. But if you prefer to take your chances—"

"Take her—take the shot one," Kenny said. "Just get my money and get me out of here!" He slammed down the phone.

Anna let out the breath she'd been holding and turned to look at Lee. He seemed to sag with relief. She had hoped she could talk some sense into him and stop this, but she now saw that it wouldn't do any good. He didn't want Lorna to die, but he obviously had lost control of what was happening here—if he'd ever had any control.

This situation was so volatile that either Lee or Kenny could set the other off. Anna realized that if Kenny really did let her and Flint take Lorna out, the rest of the SWAT team would move in right after.

"You're sending her out? She's going to die anyway," Gwendolyn screamed. "Don't you leave me here. I'm hypoglycemic. I have to eat or I'm going to be sick."

"Shut her up," Max said into Anna's ear.

"Let me see what there is to eat in this bag," Anna said, going to the one Lorna motioned to. She found the container of cookies, hesitated. Gwendolyn was working herself up again, crying and pleading for someone to do something. One cookie, mellow. Three, drunk. Six, too many.

"Would you like a cookie?" Anna asked, cringing at the thought of what she was about to do. But she had to get Gwendolyn calmed down before this escalated or the councilwoman would get them all killed.

"No!" Gwendolyn cried "I want out of here. I can't stand this any longer."

Anna practically shoved a cookie into the woman's mouth.

"I'll take one of those," Kenny said. "Don't feed them all to that sow."

Anna carried the container of cookies over to Kenny. He took one, popped it into his mouth and chewed, then spit it out with an oath. "What the hell is that taste?"

She stared at him.

"Almond," he snapped. "I hate almond flavoring."

"I'll have one," D.A. Lalane said.

Anna had been trained to save lives, not take them. She walked back over to Gwendolyn, afraid of how much of the drug Lorna had put in the cookies. If Lorna was right, one cookie wouldn't hurt them, and it might keep everyone calmer. She fed one to each of the hostages. She could hear Lorna grumbling behind her oxygen mask to give the rest to Gwendolyn.

"Give me another one," Gwendolyn demanded angrily. "You care more about a murderer than a councilwoman?"

"My job is to see that the injured victim gets the care she needs," Anna said to the councilwoman. "I'm trying to save her life. And yours. You have to be quiet."

Gwendolyn gave her a look that said she didn't have to do anything. "You tell that cop to get me out of here or else."

Anna didn't need to ask who "that cop" was. Flint. Gwendolyn had recognized him and was now threatening to blow his cover unless she was released. Anna shoved a cookie into Gwendolyn's mouth, tempted to feed her the rest.

As she turned, she could see that Kenny had heard Gwendolyn. He was frowning. She just hoped he thought the councilwoman was referring to him because of the uniform he was wearing. Clearly, Kenny didn't like Gwendolyn. He was looking at her as if he couldn't take much more of her. Anna knew the feeling.

It would seem strange not to offer Lee a cookie. He already seemed dazed and she feared that the drug might have an adverse effect, but she had to make the offer.

"Would you like a cookie?"

To her relief, he shook his head. He seemed despondent. More and more she feared that the Alzheimer's had helped him make this horrible decision and ultimately would lead him to a worse one.

"Nurse?" Flint called. "Help me take apart one of these meeting tables so we can use it as a stretcher to get the patient out."

Anna joined him in the corner, away from the others. "Gwendolyn is threatening to blow your cover," she whispered as she bent down next to him.

"I heard." He removed one of the legs from the conference table and shifted to unbolt another. "I think I can talk Kenny into letting you and Gwendolyn take Lorna out," he said. "Gwendolyn's a big woman. She should be able to help carry—"

Anna shook her head. "Send two hostages. You're going to need me—"

"Hey! No whispering over there," Kenny yelled.

They removed the other table legs and carried the top over and put it down next to Lorna.

"On the count of three," Flint said, slipping his hands under Lorna's shoulders as Anna went to her feet. "One, two, three." They lifted Lorna onto the table top, then put the oxygen tank next to her. She didn't even groan, but Anna could see that she was in terrible pain and seemed to be having more difficulty breathing.

But she was alert and staring daggers at Anna, probably because Anna hadn't given Gwendolyn enough cookies to make her comatose. Anna glanced over her shoulder at Gwendolyn. The cookies didn't seem to have had much effect. Maybe the drug was slow acting. Or maybe because of Gwendolyn's size, it took more than two cookies to mellow the woman.

"You aren't going to leave us here," Gwendolyn cried. The judge tried to hush her, but his niece hadn't paid any attention to him from the start. Anna had seen other hostages who lost control during situations like this, the stress too much for them. But she'd never come across one quite like Gwendolyn Clark.

"You can't leave us," Gwendolyn screamed. "Do something. Stop these men." She was hysterical, crying and screaming and looking right at Flint. "Isn't that what you're paid to do?"

CHAPTER NINE

1:52 p.m.

"SHUT UP!" Kenny yelled, and pulled a pistol from behind him.

Flint hadn't realized Kenny had another weapon other than the assault rifle. Kenny pointed the pistol at Gwendolyn, who was screaming, her words almost unintelligible. Almost.

"You're supposed to protect us, isn't that what you're paid to do?" Gwendolyn screamed at Flint. "Now you're just going to walk out of here and leave us?"

Anna rushed to the woman, knowing now that Gwendolyn was determined to blow Flint's cover and get him killed—if Kenny didn't shoot her first. She practically stuffed a third cookie into the woman's mouth.

"Get out of the way!" Kenny was yelling at Anna. Lee was trying to grab Kenny's arm to stop him from pulling the trigger.

Anna could hear Max in her earpiece. "Quiet her down. Whatever it takes. *Anything.* She's going to get everyone in there killed."

"There is no reason to get upset here," Anna said calmly. "Everything is going to be fine." Anna turned, putting herself between Kenny and Gwendolyn. "I think we should let the councilwoman help carry Lorna out. I'll stay behind. That way I can change your bandage when the time comes."

"Get out of my way or I'll shoot you, too," Kenny snarled. "That bitch isn't going anywhere but the grave."

FLINT STEPPED BETWEEN Kenny and the two women. Kenny was just itching to kill someone. This was going to come to a head and quickly. The problem was, Lee had moved back by the door, seemingly disoriented. Flint feared that if Kenny fired that gun, there was a good chance Lee would detonate the bomb in a knee-jerk reaction.

Flint estimated how long it would take him to get to Lee if that happened. He needed to know how much time Lee had programmed between the flip of the switch and the blast. Probably not long enough for Flint to reach Lee to get him and the bomb out of the room.

Worse, there was a good chance that Flint would be wounded if Kenny started firing. But Flint stood his ground, protecting the woman he loved, his logic as fouled up as his feelings.

Anna must have seen it, too, because the damn woman stepped around him and put herself right into the line of fire.

"You don't want to shoot anyone," she said quietly to Kenny. "You don't want anything to hold up your money or the plane. Doctor, maybe if you called, you could get Kenny some pain pills. That arm must be killing him."

Flint stared at her back, wanting to throttle her. But when he looked at Kenny, he saw that he had lowered the gun, and Flint realized something that Anna obvi-

ously had seen right away. Kenny was a junkie and he
needed a fix.

"My arm *is* killing me." Kenny glanced at Gwendolyn, daring her to make a sound, but didn't raise the gun.

Flint couldn't believe the way Anna had handled the
situation. His heart was pounding, his legs were weak.
He watched Anna, awestruck by how calm she appeared,
how well she was handling Kenny, handling all of them.

Kenny had the gun resting on his thigh now. He
seemed to have backed off. For the moment. Flint had
to get Anna and as many of the hostages out of here as
he could. But he was aware he couldn't take down
Kenny and disarm the bomb on Lee by himself.

He knew Max would take advantage of the situation
when the door opened again. Anna seemed to know it,
as well. This wasn't what Flint had hoped for, but there
was no way to contain this situation other than by force.
The next step was to get Lorna out of here and to use
that diversion to do a full breach.

Meanwhile he had to start thinking like the SWAT
team commander he was, not the lovesick fool he'd
been. Anna was right, he had to admit. He needed her
if he hoped to stop these two. The thought killed him.
If he hoped to do his job, he had to keep Anna here with
him. He couldn't do it without her. Once the team went
full breach, he needed Anna to take down Kenny while
he took care of Lee and the bomb.

He looked over at her. She seemed so fearless now,
but by their second date, Flint had known something was
wrong. Anna had seemed afraid of intimacy. Not afraid.
Terrified. At first he'd thought it was just him. He did

come on too strong—especially when he wanted something. Also, he was a lot larger than she was, stronger, and he'd worried that he somehow frightened her.

But he'd been smart enough not to question her about it. Instead he'd done everything possible to make her feel comfortable around him. He'd known he had to move slowly, carefully.

Still, he couldn't help but wonder what it was that had frightened her so much. A love affair gone wrong? Something had happened to make her afraid of men, and Flint had been determined to find out what it was and to help Anna get over it. And Anna had seemed just as determined to keep whatever it was a secret.

2:14 p.m.

"CALM DOWN. Everything is going to be fine." Anna spoke loud enough for everyone in the room to hear as she met Kenny's gaze. She couldn't believe Flint. He'd tried to protect her. What if Lee had flipped the switch on the bomb? There was no way Flint could have gotten to him in time. And what if Kenny had shot him? Where would that have left them all?

She'd feared this might happen. That Flint would be so busy trying to protect her that he would forget his job. She shot him a look. His chastised expression made it clear he'd realized what he'd done. If everything went wild in here, he couldn't protect her even if he tried. She saw that in his eyes, the pain, the realization.

She could feel the rampant beat of her heart as she met his gaze. They both knew it would be hell getting out of here alive unless they could get everyone quieted down and do their jobs, forgetting what had once been between them.

"If you can talk your way out with Lorna, I want you out of there, Anna," Max said into her earpiece. "That's an order."

Anna could feel Flint's gaze, warm on her skin. She looked up into his eyes. Max hadn't said anything about Flint going out with them. Just the thought of leaving him here in this room was too much for her. She understood his need to protect her too well. She had to find a way to get them all out of here. She couldn't leave Flint. He wouldn't be able to neutralize two men, especially these two men, alone. Even if he could disarm the bomb in time, someone needed to make sure that Kenny wasn't going to slow him down. That someone was going to be her. Come hell or high water.

If any more shots were fired, she knew Max would go tactical real quickly, sending in the SWAT team, guns blazing in the hopes of saving as many of them as possible.

She'd seen this sort of thing in Washington, D.C., a few years ago. The team had come in and literally thrown the subject wearing the bomb out the window. The area below had been cleared for just such a maneuver. The man had already activated the device before going out the window. The bomb had exploded between the fourth and third floors on his way down. It had taken out all the windows on that side of the building, but the hostages were unharmed. The man wearing the bomb was lost in the explosion.

Anna knew that was exactly what Flint had been ordered to do.

"I can't take this anymore," Gwendolyn cried, sounding a little drunk. The cookies weren't acting quickly enough. Anna had to shut the woman up.

She stuffed another cookie into Gwendolyn's mouth and, trying to keep her voice calm, said, "Doctor, could you toss me the tape from my bag." She just hoped four cookies didn't kill the woman.

Gwendolyn's eyes were like saucers as she looked up at Anna, obviously suspecting what she had in mind. The councilwoman frantically tried to swallow the cookie. It was clear that once she did, Gwendolyn was going to blow Flint's cover and do even more damage. The stress of this situation aside, this was a woman who was used to getting her way, no matter who got hurt in the process.

"Here," Flint said, but instead of tossing her the tape, he brought it over to her. His fingers brushed hers as he handed her the tape, and she felt heat ripple through her, warming her skin.

Do Whatever It Takes. Wasn't that what his T-shirt had said? Her stomach knotted at the thought that she might have created this man. He had wanted to be chief of police when they'd been together. All her talk of SWAT, was that why he was now the head of the Courage Bay team? He had been risking his life since she'd left him and she suspected it was for all the wrong reasons. And now he was ready to take a bullet for her without even considering his own life.

What surprised her was that she felt the same way.

All that telling herself she was over Flint Mauro—well, it had obviously been a lie. The feelings were still there. So were the reasons they couldn't be together. Reasons she had magnified by taking this job.

But they were on the same team now. In this together in a way they hadn't been when they were engaged. And that made her feel closer to Flint than she had before.

The moment Gwendolyn swallowed the last of the cookie, Flint helped Anna tape her mouth with several pieces of tape as the councilwoman struggled, her eyes glaring holes into Flint and Anna. If looks could kill, they'd both be dead. Ditto if Gwendolyn managed to get the tape off.

"You are going to get us all killed if you don't shut up," Anna whispered as she applied more tape.

Two large tears coursed down the woman's cheek. Hatred radiated from her eyes as she struggled against the tape on her mouth, desperate to rat them all out, wanting blood, just not her own.

I will get you fired, the look said as she glanced from Flint to Anna and back.

"Better than getting us *killed,*" Anna whispered.

Gwendolyn was struggling to get the tape off her mouth, her eyes mean with anger and open threats. Anna reached for one of the medical bags. As much as she hated to do this, she was going to have to give the councilwoman something to settle her down.

She pulled out a vial of a drug that should put Gwendolyn Clark out like a light. Add the four cookies and whatever drug was in there— Because of the woman's size, Anna had a feeling it would take an elephant dart to put Gwendolyn down. But still, in good conscience Anna decided to cut down the dosage. She didn't want to kill Gwendolyn, just shut her up.

FLINT SAW WHAT Anna planned to do and turned a little to shield her actions from Lee and Kenny. The two men couldn't have been more dissimilar. Kenny wanted money and a plane and a passport. Lee just wanted someone to validate his pain. Flint feared the homemade bomb taped to the older man's chest was the way Lee planned to get that validation—not on some video on the nightly news.

At first Flint hadn't understood what would make a quiet, law-abiding, educated man like Lee Harper duct-tape a homemade bomb to himself. He could understand taking over city hall—even as desperate and futile as that was.

But the bomb had thrown Flint until he'd met Kenny. Then Flint had understood. The older man had known his partner was a loose cannon. Lee had taken things into his own hands, building the bomb, knowing it would trump anything that Kenny tried to threaten him with. This would end when Lee said it would—and the way he'd planned it. And there was nothing Kenny could do about it.

Flint wondered if he and Anna would be able to do anything about that, either, as he looked at Lee. The man had his finger on the switch and there was something deadly and final in his filmy gaze.

Flint looked at Anna. She was something. What a re-markable woman. That alone added to his fear that someone as unique and wonderful as Anna might not see another sunrise if things went badly in this room.

He would protect her to his death, he thought, and smiled to himself. Thank God he hadn't let her come in here alone. He couldn't bear the thought of watching all of this on the video at the Incident Command Center.

Together they just might be able to pull this off. He had to hang on to that hope. He couldn't contemplate the alternative. They would do their jobs, because as Max said, they were the best at what they did. Anna sure as hell was, he thought grudgingly. She was flat amazing. Max had been right in his appraisal of her. Flint couldn't imagine what would have happened in this room if she hadn't been here.

Now, if only Kenny kept his part of the bargain and let them take Lorna out. He turned so no one could see him signal Max that it was almost time to go full breach. Flint felt his heart pound a little harder. Once SWAT went tactical, he and Anna would really be on their own.

2:33 p.m.

SEEING THE NEEDLE and realizing what Anna had in mind, Gwendolyn kicked out at her. Anna moved to the side and shoved up the sleeve of the woman's cotton shirt as Gwendolyn fought her.

"What are you doing?" Kenny demanded, suddenly appearing next to her after he shoved Flint aside with the assault rifle. He held the pistol in his other hand at his side.

"Just trying to calm down the councilwoman," Anna said without looking at him as she hurriedly jabbed the needle into Gwendolyn's arm. The woman let out of a muffled howl behind the tape on her mouth.

"I thought you didn't have any real drugs in there?" Kenny said, suspicion in his voice.

"Nothing for *pain*," Anna told him. "This should put Ms. Clark out for a little while." Gwendolyn was glaring daggers and working furiously to get the tape off her mouth before the drug could take effect.

Anna turned to look at Kenny. "I didn't think you would want that sort of side effect."

Kenny nodded, though he still looked suspicious as he stared down at the councilwoman. Then he turned to look back at Lee and Flint. Lee was standing over by the door, his finger on the toggle switch to the bomb. Flint had moved over by Lorna on the makeshift stretcher.

"Sit down," Kenny ordered Flint, who squatted next to Lorna and pretended to check her vitals. "Tape the rest of the hostages's mouths, then sit down," Kenny said to Anna.

She did as he ordered, then quickly went to join Flint and Lorna, afraid Kenny would try to separate her from Flint.

As she checked Lorna's vitals herself, she glanced at the hostages. They all looked calmer. Gwendolyn looked smashed, eyes unfocused, zoning out. *Finally* silent.

Lorna moved her oxygen mask aside. "Gwendolyn's an idiot," Lorna whispered. "I'm surprised she didn't get us all killed. Someone ought to put that woman to sleep."

Anna wasn't surprised at Lorna's suggestion, given what she knew about the cookies. She had to admit she'd wanted to ring Gwendolyn's neck herself. The councilwoman had almost blown Flint's cover—and had definitely put all their lives at risk, especially Flint's.

"She only got elected because she was related to the judge," Lorna whispered.

Apparently, Gwendolyn had ears like a cat and the constitution of a Mack truck. She raised her head and glared at Lorna even in her drunken state. She mumbled something behind the tape, but the only distinguishable part was "my uncle the judge's help."

The councilwoman had worked a small hole in between the strips of tape with her tongue.

Kenny looked up, his eyes widening as if a light had come on. He walked over to Gwendolyn and ripped off the tape. She let out a yelp and called him a bastard.

"The judge is your uncle?" he asked her.

Judge Craven was trying to shush her from behind his tape, but Gwendolyn was having none of it.

"That's right," the councilwoman said, her words slurring, but still clear enough that they all understood. "I'm Judge Lawrence Craven's niece. You have no idea who you're messing with. My uncle will see that you rot in prison, if not go to the electric chair."

"Shut up, you stupid woman," Lorna rasped.

"If you don't die, I'll get you fired," Gwendolyn said, glaring over at her.

"Have another cookie, Gwendolyn."

Gwendolyn narrowed her gaze suspiciously. "You put something in the cookies."

Yes, Anna thought, but what had Lorna planned? Surely not to kill the woman. Given what Anna knew about Lorna, she suspected the cookies had been more to discredit the councilwoman. Maybe a drunk-driving charge, since Gwendolyn would have appeared intoxicated after eating a few.

Anna wanted to believe that had been all Lorna had planned. Not murder.

Not that it mattered anymore. Both women had worse to worry about than their plots against each other.

The phone rang.

"Look, I'm tired of waiting," Kenny barked into the receiver. "If you don't meet my demands, I'm going to kill the judge's niece."

"Good choice," Lorna whispered, pulling aside the oxygen mask again.

Anna put it back in place and motioned for Lorna to keep quiet.

Gwendolyn looked up and tried to focus on Kenny as he went to stand over her. The judge was trying to say something from behind the tape over his mouth.

"You hear me?" Kenny screamed into the phone. "No, don't give me any more excuses!" He slammed down the phone and looked around the room as if daring anyone to say a word or he would shoot them.

"You promised to send out the woman and the video camera," Lee said.

Kenny glared at him, but said nothing.

2:42 p.m.

"IT'S TIME," Flint whispered to Anna. He looked into her eyes and knew she understood perfectly. This situation had reached the point where they had to make a move now.

"I'll take care of Kenny," she whispered.

Flint nodded, feeling his heart rate pick up. He was worried about what she had in mind.

"Stop whispering over there," Kenny yelled to them.

Flint leaned back against the wall. Anna sat on the other side of Lorna and continued to monitor her patient.

Kenny paced back and forth against the far wall, his gaze moving from Lee to the hostages to Flint and Anna. His expression soured at the sight of Lorna.

Flint let his focus return to Anna. She was so beautiful. He'd thought his memory had been prejudiced by his love for her. But he was wrong. She was even more exquisite than he remembered. There was a softness to her face as she took Lorna's blood pressure, her hands so sure.

He had known by his second date with Anna that he wanted to marry her. He'd been smart enough to keep that knowledge to himself. His friends would have thought he was crazy. He didn't even know this woman, they would have argued.

But he did know her. He could feel a connection between them that was so strong it made his knees weak. Except Anna was keeping him at arm's length emotionally. Sure, she accepted his dates. They would talk and laugh and kiss, but he could feel the wall she had erected between them.

Flint was determined to tear down that wall even if he had to do it brick by brick. He knew he had to gain her trust to get to the reason for her reserve, her terror of men. So he bided his time. He didn't push. He waited.

It wasn't easy. He wanted to call her parents and try to find out what had happened to Anna to make her this way. He did find out that she hadn't dated much. She said she'd been too busy going to college, training to become a paramedic, too busy working after that.

He didn't buy it. Not a woman who looked like Anna.

When Anna's mother called to invite him to Sunday dinner, he was delighted. But when he told Anna, her reaction surprised him. She was angry and upset.

"My mother just wants to interrogate you," Anna said. "You don't know what she's like."

No, he didn't. When one of his brothers had come through town, Flint had made sure Anna got to meet him. He wanted his whole family to meet Anna, but they lived all over the country. Her parents lived right here in town and she hadn't ever suggested taking him home to meet them.

"If you want me to, I'll call your mom and tell her I can't make it," he said.

Anna looked over at him, tears glistening in her eyes. "No," she said, and moved to him, cupping his face in her hands. "No. I've been wanting you to meet my dad."

He felt as though he'd just scaled Mt. Everest. "Great. I'd love to meet him, and don't worry about your mother. She can interrogate me all she wants. Really."

Anna only nodded. "With my luck, my sister Emily and her husband Lance will be there, too."

He lifted her chin to look into her beautiful eyes. "I don't mind meeting your sister Emily and her husband Lance."

"You can say that now," she said.

He laughed. "Wait until you meet my brother Curtis. His idea of dressing up is putting on his cleanest overalls. Did I mention he raises pigs out in Michigan?"

"There is nothing wrong with raising pigs or wearing overalls," she said indignantly.

"I know," he said, laughing. He'd pulled her into his arms. "But when we have dinner, he always has to tell me the name of the pig we're eating at the time."

She laughed then, not sure if he was serious or not. "Thank you."

"I haven't done anything," he said.

"Yes, you have. You just don't know it."

"ANNA," Max said in her ear. "I want you and Flint out of there. Try to get Kenny to let you take out the wounded woman now. Once through the door, the team will move in."

She nodded slowly and held up her fingers to answer yes, then took a deep breath, her gaze going to the hostages. Gwendolyn Clark was staring at her. Even as drugged as she was, the councilwoman had seen Anna nod and recognized her action as some type of signal.

Gwendolyn was obviously dying to tell Kenny. Maybe she thought the information could buy her a way out of here.

When Anna looked over at the judge, she saw that he, too, knew what was going on. He nodded and closed his eyes, no doubt assuming Anna's signal would put an end to this one way or another.

The phone rang. Kenny picked it up, grimaced in pain and let out a string of obscenities.

"I just wanted to let you know we are getting what you asked for, but I need a show of faith from you," Anna heard Max say through her earpiece. "Give me the wounded hostage and I'll try to get things moving faster."

Kenny let out an oath and slammed down the phone.

"You want me to look at your arm?" Anna asked quietly as she got up and started toward him. She heard Flint's softly spoken oath behind her. Her heart was pounding so hard she feared he could hear. She licked her lips, her mouth dry. "You might have gotten it bleeding again."

"No, you've done enough damage." He took a couple of deep breaths. "I've got to have something for this pain."

Anna nodded, having been waiting for this. "I can have the doctor call or I can see about getting you something." She motioned to the phone.

He looked at her as if he wondered how she thought she could get him drugs when he had a half dozen hostages and he couldn't get squat.

"May I try?" she asked.

"Whatever." He turned away in disgust. "Just get me something to take the edge off the pain." He turned back to her. "Nothing so strong it knocks me out, or you'll be the person I shoot before I go down, got it?"

She nodded. She understood a lot more than he knew. She saw that it wasn't the pain in his arm that he needed the drugs for. He looked like some of the strung-out addicts she'd dealt with in D.C. Edgy and unpredictable. Only one thing on their minds: their next fix.

Kenny's "fix" was the prescription drugs his sister used to obtain for him.

"I could see if I can get you some OxyContin," she said, pronouncing it "oxycotton" like on the street.

He turned to look at her, his mood picking up. "Like they're going to give you the drugs. They haven't given me anything I've asked for. I guess I'm going to have to start killing people. Maybe then they'll take me seriously."

"I can tell them that we have to have the drugs within the next thirty minutes," she suggested.

He eyed her. "Like they'll listen to you."

She lifted a brow. "I'm a woman and a nurse. Women can be more persuasive than men. Even doctors." She already knew that Kenny was a raving chauvinist. It went without saying that he thought women had it easier than men in his world. "Women have their ways."

"You'll need a doctor's signature to get a prescription," Flint said, sounding very much like a doctor.

She shook her head, still focusing on Kenny. "The police chief will figure it out."

Kenny smiled ruefully at that, then looked her over. "You married?"

She could feel Flint's gaze on her as she shook her head. "I came close once."

"Yeah, me, too." Kenny still didn't trust her his expression said. "You wouldn't be trying to pull something, would you?"

She shook her head slowly. "I just need to convince the police chief that we have a better chance of getting out of here safely if you're comfortable and not in pain."

He still looked doubtful. He was sweating, his face flushed. He needed the drugs and soon.

Anna hoped Max was already getting the prescription filled. "The police might have enough time to get the pills before your helicopter gets here. Otherwise, you might have to make the trip without them. But if you'd rather have the doctor try…" She turned to go back over by Lorna and Flint.

She knew Kenny was imagining flying to another country in a fancy private jet, high on his favorite drug, rich and looking forward to his dream future.

His need for the drugs was strong. But so was his fear that a mistake would land him in prison or a cemetery. She turned to give him a tired, bored look, as if it didn't matter one way or the other to her.

Kenny glanced toward the phone, then motioned her over to it with his gun. "But if you do anything or say anything you aren't supposed to…"

She just nodded and picked up the receiver. She almost dialed the incident command number. Instead she looked at him. "Is there some way to reach them or should I dial 911?"

He seemed to relax a little, relieved she hadn't known the number, as if that renewed his faith that she was no more than a nurse, and nurses were safe. "Here's the number the cop gave me."

"Nice work," Max said into her earpiece as she dialed the number Kenny had scribbled on a scrap of paper. "We're getting the prescription filled. Try to stall him as long as you can."

"This is Anna Carson," she said when Max answered. "I'm the nurse inside city hall. I'm going to need a prescription filled for my patient." She looked up. "Kenny, is there anything you're allergic to? Any medications you've taken before and had side effects?"

"Nah, nothing."

"Is there any drug you're currently taking?" she asked.

"Just get me some damned painkillers," he snapped.

"I have to ask these questions," she said, unruffled. "Sometimes if you've taken something for a long time and you take something else, it can kill you."

That stopped him. He rattled off a long list of prescription painkillers he took, depending on whatever his sister had been able to get for him.

She nodded. "No adverse side effects?"

He gave her a look like she had to be kidding. "Tell them to hurry with the drugs or I'm going to start shooting. I'm sick of them, okay?"

"Okay." Then into the phone, she said, "I need Oxy-Contin. Do you need me to spell the name of the drug for you?" She gave Kenny a look like "dumb cops."

He chuckled and shook his head.

Anna spelled the name out, then gave the dosage required. She looked over at Flint. He was watching Lee. She'd almost forgotten about Lee. Almost. He seemed to be lost in a daze, distancing himself from everything that was happening in this room.

When she looked back at Flint, he winked at her. Her heart did a small roller-coaster loop in her chest as she held his gaze for a moment.

"Tell 'em to leave the drugs outside the door," Kenny said.

"Yes, just leave them outside the door," she told Max.

"Tell him I'm doing everything you've asked," Max instructed. "Can you get Lorna out?"

Anna looked at Kenny. "He said he would get it right away if we release Lorna Sinke." She used "We," wanting him to feel she was in this with him. Her look said, *Why not? Let's humor them.* She glanced at Lorna.

Kenny shook his head. His gaze scanned the hostages, halting on Flint. He didn't like Flint's size and he no longer needed a doctor.

Anna held her breath. Kenny shifted his attention to Gwendolyn Clark. She looked completely out of it, finally.

"Give them Lorna," Lee said, startling them both. Kenny's head jerked around. Clearly he didn't like Lee giving him orders. The two glared at each other across the room.

Anna moved closer to Kenny and whispered, "Let them have Lorna. She isn't going to make it anyway." It was a lie. Lorna was strong and tough. She should make it if Anna could get her to a hospital. But Kenny didn't know that. "That way, when she does die, it won't be here. It will be better for you, you know."

He glanced over at Lorna. Lorna had her eyes closed. "Fine, trade her. But I want those drugs and I want them now."

"It will take two hostages to carry her out," Anna said, hoping he went for it. She didn't dare look in Flint's direction.

"That wasn't the plan," Max said into her ear. "I want you out of there."

Kenny stood staring at Lee as if waiting for Lee to give him another order. There was a tightness to his mouth that Lee must have noticed, as well. When Lee didn't say anything, Kenny said, "Take the lawyers. No one cares if attorneys die." He indicated the district attorney and city attorney.

Lee reached into his pocket with his free hand and held out the keys to the handcuffs.

"Lorna's coming out with the lawyers," Anna said into the phone and hung up. As she reached for the handcuff keys, her fingers were trembling. If she could just get three of them out of here without another incident...

She moved to the two attorneys and uncuffed them. Both rubbed their wrists and quickly got to their feet, moving toward the makeshift stretcher Lorna lay on. Anna went over to check her patient. Lorna was still hanging in. Anna couldn't believe how tough she was as she checked her pulse one last time.

Lorna reached up to pull aside the oxygen. "Thank you." The mask fell back into place. Anna met the woman's gaze, held it for a moment, then nodded for the men to carry her out.

Lee moved to push aside the desk blocking the door. The D.A. and city attorney lifted the table with the injured woman on it. Anna steadied the oxygen and walked as far as the door with them. She could feel the assault rifle on them, Kenny watching every move. Was he really going to let them leave?

She was afraid something would happen at the last moment to keep the three hostages from getting out.

The D.A. and city attorney waited as Lee unlocked the door and opened it a crack. Anna could see that the hallway was empty. But she knew the SWAT team was there, ready. She prayed nothing happened to keep Lorna and the two attorneys from getting through that door.

She let go of the oxygen tank as the men started

through the opening with Lorna on the makeshift stretcher. Just a few more feet and they would be out.

"Just a minute," Kenny said behind Anna.

CHAPTER TEN

3:11 p.m.

FLINT KNEW WHY Kenny had stopped them. He'd heard the councilwoman. She'd obviously come to and seen what was happening.

Flint had been watching Kenny's eyes. He saw the slight change in the man's manner, recognized it and knew just an instant before Kenny pulled the trigger that he'd heard Councilwoman Gwendolyn Clark say, "They're cops!"

Shoving himself off the wall, Flint dived toward Kenny.

The blast of the assault rifle exploded in the room, thundering off the walls as bullets riddled the plaster just past Anna and Lee.

The sound of the gunshot reverberated through his head as he struggled on the floor with Kenny, trying to get the rifle away before Kenny could get another shot off. Kenny was stronger than he looked. It wasn't until Flint heard the report, felt the searing ball of fire burn through his flesh that he realized Kenny had pulled the pistol and fired.

"No!" ANNA CRIED as all hell broke loose, just as she'd feared. The D.A. and city attorney lunged out the doorway at a run with the stretcher.

Behind her, Anna heard Flint come off the wall and hit Kenny, heard the rifle hit the floor and the two of them scuffling. Anna saw the expression on Lee's face. Her gaze locked with his and she pleaded silently for him not to flip that switch.

From outside the room came the quickened beat of footfalls as the attorneys ran down the hall with the makeshift litter and Lorna, and the SWAT team burst out from where they had been waiting.

Everything happened so fast, she didn't have time to take a breath. Before the SWAT team could get past the makeshift stretcher held by the two attorneys, Lee had slammed the door and shoved the barricade against it, all the time keeping his finger on the bomb switch.

The first shot had startled her. The second one turned her blood to ice. She spun around, the report still echoing in the room. Kenny was on his knees, holding the pistol to Flint's head. "Call them off!" he screamed. "Or I'll kill the cop."

The SWAT team rammed the door. Anna knew any moment they would be dropping in from the ceiling.

"Hold your position," Anna yelled. "Officer down. Hold your position."

The battering of the door stopped. She thought she heard a creak overhead. She held her breath, staring at Flint. He was sprawled on the floor, his shirt dark with blood, his eyes closed.

In the deafening silence that fell over the room, Kenny slowly straightened, his face twisted in anger.

Anna thought for a moment he would shoot her, as well. Kenny stared at her, the gun raised, his hand shaking with what she could only assume was rage. The man wasn't stupid. He'd known a trap had been set for him when the hostages were released. That would be the last of them to leave this room alive, Anna thought.

She looked past Kenny to Flint, praying he wasn't seriously injured. She'd stopped the breach to save his life, and now realized that decision might have been at the cost of all their lives.

"Is Flint alive?" Max said in her ear as she stepped past Kenny and dropped to her knees beside the only man she'd ever loved.

3:24 p.m.

FLINT HAD A FLASH of memory as painful as the bullet that had torn through his flesh. The morning he was six and his mother had walked down to the corner market to get milk. Her husband had already gone to work so she'd left Flint's older brother Curtis in charge of everyone. She had gone to the corner store before and knew she wouldn't be gone but a few minutes.

A teenager with a gun was robbing the market when she walked in the door. The kid panicked, turned and shot. She died instantly.

Flint didn't know why he had to think about that morning now. Maybe because he associated all pain with the loss of his mother that day. It was impossible for a kid of six to understand why things like that happened. It was still hard for a man of thirty-four to accept that kind of loss.

His father had done a great job caring for five kids by himself, but Flint had sworn that his children would have a mother to raise them to adulthood—the one thing he had envied his friends and Anna.

She had the kind of family he'd always wanted; a mother, father, a stable household and only one sibling. He'd had four brothers, way too many when he was the youngest. Anna's life had sounded like heaven to him. He'd imagined the house Anna had been raised in and wasn't surprised that Sunday when he'd gone there for dinner to see that he'd been right.

It was a *Leave It to Beaver* kind of house in a classic neighborhood where men mowed their lawns on Saturday afternoons and kids played ball in the quiet street and mothers made pot roasts for dinner and baked homemade pie for dessert.

But the moment he'd walked in that door so many Sundays ago, he'd understood some of Anna's reservations about his meeting the family.

Mary Louise Carson was nothing like her daughter. She was tall and gangly, cold and distant. There was something brittle about her, an edge. She did interrogate him, but not out of interest, he thought. She seemed to be looking for his flaws.

Anna's father, Bob Carson, was a warm, nice man, quiet but interested, and obviously a huge fan of Anna's.

Emily and her husband Lance were reserved at best, suspicious at worst. It made Flint wonder if Anna had

had another boyfriend before him, one who had caused all this distrust.

"Does your family live around here?" Anna's mother asked after they'd taken a seat in the living room.

Flint shook his head. "My mother was killed when I was six."

"Oh, I'm so sorry," she said, and shot a look at her husband.

"It was tough growing up without a mother," he said. "But my father was in construction and he worked very hard and we never went hungry. There was a bunch of us, so he had to work a lot." He laughed. "I was the youngest of five boys. I always wondered what it would be like to get all new clothes when mine wore out."

Everyone chuckled at that. But he could see that Mary Louise thought him from poor stock in more ways than one.

"Your father raised you five boys," Bob said. "You must be very proud of him."

"I am," Flint replied. "He really did work to be both father and mother to us. The older boys helped. I was the youngest, so I had to learn to be pretty tough to survive." He stopped and looked up from his plate. "Don't get me wrong. It was a lot of fun. You can't believe the pillow fights we used to have." He'd laughed and the mood lightened a little.

"Is your father still alive?" Bob asked.

Shaking his head, Flint said, "He died the year after I became a police officer. I was glad he at least got to see me in uniform."

"Do your brothers live around here?" her mother asked.

"They're all over the country," he told her. "We get together for weddings and funerals, that's about it. I'd always hoped we would live closer so we could have those big family get-togethers." He glanced at Anna. "I guess I'm going to have to make my own big family."

Mary Louise made a distasteful face and asked about his job and his plans for the future.

Anna changed the subject and, after dinner, she excused herself to give Flint a tour of the house and backyard.

"I told you it would be horrible," she said. "I'm sorry."

"It wasn't horrible," he said, and pulled her behind an apple tree to give her a kiss.

She looked into his eyes, her gaze softening. "My dad likes you."

"That's good, right?"

"That's very good," she said.

"Anna, sometime will you tell me why everyone, you included, is so suspicious of me?"

Her smile faded. "It's not you."

"Whatever it is, will you tell me?"

"Sometime."

That's why he'd blown it with Anna, he thought now. Because he'd had an image in his head all these years of this perfect family he would build, as if he could remake history, have his mother back, change everything. He'd thought he could make his own family with Anna. He hadn't considered how Anna's own past would play into their future.

"Flint—Flint?" she whispered next to him now. Something warm and wet splashed against his cheek

and ran down his neck to his shirt. He opened his eyes
and saw that she was crying softly.

She backhanded her tears as she worked, dragging
one of the medical bags over to her. "You're going to
be fine," she said. "Just fine. You hear me?"

3:29 p.m.

KENNY STORMED OVER to Gwendolyn and jerked her head
up by her hair. The councilwoman let out a shriek of pain.

"What did you say?" he demanded.

Lee was mumbling in the background, "I told you not
to shoot anyone."

Gwendolyn was still shrieking, sounding more angry
than hurt.

"What did you say about *cops?*" Kenny slapped her,
startling her into silence for an instant. "What did you
say?" he demanded, pointing the gun between her eyes.

Gwendolyn's gaze jerked from Kenny to Flint, then
Anna. "They're cops."

Kenny stared at her for a long moment, then turned
slowly to look at Anna, his gaze so filled with hate, it
took all of her willpower not to flinch.

"You're a cop?" he asked, daring her to deny it.

"I'm a SWAT team paramedic," she said.

"What the hell is that?" he asked.

"I'm sent in to help the victims of situations like this."

He swung his gaze to Flint on the floor. "You're not
a doctor. You're a cop, too."

"His name is Flint Mauro," Anna said.

"He's the head of the SWAT team," Gwendolyn blurted,

then looked at Anna as if to say, *There, that pays you back for taping my mouth and injecting me with something.*

Kenny was shaking his head as if in disbelief that Flint and Anna had thought they could get away with this. "You came in here to do what exactly?"

"To help the injured," Anna said.

Kenny shot her a get-real look. "You came in here to stop me."

"We came in to try to keep anyone else from getting hurt," she explained.

"And you've done one hell of a job," Kenny said. He looked at Flint. "You got yourself shot. And *you*—" He turned to Anna. "You got the council aide out of here, didn't you? Too bad you weren't smart enough to get you and your buddy out of here, too. Move out of the way. He's a dead man."

Anna stood slowly, blocking Flint's body with her own as she moved closer to Kenny and lowered her voice. "You kill either of us and you will never see the money or the plane. The only reason the SWAT team isn't swarming this room right now is because I stopped them."

She saw the hesitation in his eyes. He must have remembered her calling out, "Hold your positions."

"If you fire another shot," Anna said, "I won't be able to stop them. I don't think I need to tell you what will happen." She glanced over at Lee, who was visibly shaking, his finger still on that damned switch. "If you want out of here alive, you won't kill anyone."

The phone began to ring.

Anna held her breath, afraid it would stop after the first ring, a signal that Max intended to go to a full breach. When the phone rang again, she felt sick with relief.

Gwendolyn started crying again, a drunken kind of wallowing-in-self-pity sound.

"You shot him," Lee was still saying. "This is not what I wanted. Not this. Not any of this."

"Shut up," Kenny ordered, his voice sounding almost normal as he ignored the phone and walked past them to peer out through the blinds. He was careful to keep his body behind the wall, careful not to let the marksmen across the street get a shot. "Everyone just shut up."

Then he walked to the phone and picked it up. "Get me what I want now or I'm going to kill them all."

3:32 p.m.

"TALK TO ME," Anna said as blood bloomed through the fabric of Flint's shirt. She knelt beside him and lifted his shirt. He'd been hit in the side, away from any vital organs, but he'd lost a lot of blood already.

Hurriedly she applied pressure to the wound to stop the bleeding, digging with her hand for the trauma dressings and bandages in the medical bag. She tried to lose herself in the motions. *Don't think about this being Flint. Just do your job.*

But then she met his gaze and her eyes burned with tears at the sight of him wounded, hurt, in pain.

Flint was looking up at her, smiling. "You are something, you know that?"

"It's the pain talking," she said as she worked to stop

the bleeding, pulling herself together, not wanting him to see how vulnerable she was when it came to him.

Behind her she could hear Kenny on the phone, his anger growing as time passed.

"Unhook the brace," he whispered.

She frowned down at him.

He winked. "I'm going to need all the mobility I can get."

He didn't really believe he could do anything after this injury, did he? What was she thinking? He was Flint Mauro. The Do Whatever It Takes guy.

"I'm going to have to take your brace off," she said, loud enough that Kenny could hear her. She could feel him watching her.

Flint groaned as if in pain and closed his eyes. She took off the brace, wondering if the groan was real or for Kenny's benefit.

When he opened his eyes, she said, "I think the bullet went all the way through."

"That's nice," he said.

She stared into his handsome face, fighting tears. She had to get him out of here. Had to get him to a hospital.

"Don't look so worried," he said, watching her closely. Too closely. "I've been wounded worse than this."

The tears welled and spilled. He'd been wounded more seriously in the years she'd been gone? She hadn't even known. He could have died and she wouldn't have known.

"I don't think you should try to get up," she whispered.

He smiled. "I can walk. Don't worry."

It killed her to see him shot, in pain, bleeding. But if he couldn't walk, it would be hell getting him out of here.

"If you're thinking of trading me for the pills, forget it," Flint said. "He's not going to let a cop leave here and you know it."

That's exactly what she'd been thinking, but she knew he was right. She finished bandaging his side. The bleeding had stopped. As long as he didn't move—

"Don't worry about me," Flint said. "Kenny will let you leave for the pills. Make the exchange."

She shook her head. "I'm not leaving you. Once Kenny gets the pills, we wait for them to work." If Kenny didn't kill them all before that. "It will be my best chance of getting close enough to disarm him."

Flint looked as if he wanted to argue, but the cop in him had to know that that was the only way out of this. There was no talking either Lee or Kenny down.

"I'll do my part, count on it," Flint said, obviously trying to hide the pain from her.

She knew he would at least kill himself trying.

Behind her, Kenny quit yelling into the phone at Max and slammed down the receiver.

A tentative knock sounded on the door. The pills. She closed her eyes for a moment in thanks, then stood and turned, still shielding Flint's body just in case Kenny was thinking of finishing him off.

"That will be your pills," she said.

Kenny looked at her for a long moment. Another knock. Then another.

She could see his need to kill someone weighed against his need for the pills. Clearly he wanted to turn the assault rifle on the door and kill the messenger. Or at least kill Flint. But maybe Kenny had taken her warning to heart. At the very least, the last thing he wanted was for the person at the door to leave. He could always get the pills and then kill someone.

"Go to the door," he said, motioning to her. "I'll be right behind you." He stepped up, poking her in the back with the rifle barrel. She sent a warning glance to Flint as she moved to the door and shoved the desk aside.

Lee, to her surprise, moved out of the way as Kenny pushed her toward the door. She watched him, suspecting he would be upset about Kenny taking the drugs, maybe even worried.

But his face was expressionless, his gaze on Flint. He seemed to expect trouble would be coming from that direction when it came. Smart man.

"Open the door…slowly," Kenny ordered.

Anna did as she was told. She could see movement on the other side through the hole in the door. She started to reach to open the door, but Kenny stopped her.

"On second thought, tell them to just put the package through the hole," he said.

Anna reached through the hole. It was just large enough for her hand. She felt the container of pills drop into her palm. Slowly she pulled them back. Turning, she met Kenny's gaze and held the drugs out.

He grabbed the container and motioned for her to push the desk back across the door.

"I'd be careful taking these," she warned after she'd barricaded the door under his watchful eye. She'd ordered him a much stronger dosage than he usually took. One would knock someone Kenny's size on his ass.

But she knew Kenny's body had probably built up a resistance to the drug. He would require a higher dosage just to take the edge off the pain. She was also counting on him downing extra pills because he hadn't had them for a while. "I wouldn't take more than two of those at a time."

"I'm sure you wouldn't," he said, sticking the pistol into the waist of his uniform and laying the assault rifle on a chair next to him to free up his hands. He fought to open the container. "Damned child-proof caps."

She held out her hand.

He stared at it, then her, and tried to strong-arm the lid off the container, causing more pain to his shoulder. In frustration, he shoved the container of pills at her.

She opened the lid easily and removed the cotton before handing it back to him. The container was filled with pills.

He stared down at them as if in awe, then motioned her away, waiting until she was at Flint's side, kneeling on the floor next to him, before he looked lovingly at the pills again, then spilled three into his hand and swallowed them dry, closing his eyes.

His entire body stilled. Anna looked at Flint. He shook his head, shifting just slightly. She knew he was as impatient as she was, but he agreed her plan to wait for the pills to act was the best one.

Kenny's eyes flew open and he glared at Flint. He expected Flint to try something. He would be waiting for it now that he knew Flint was the head of SWAT. Anna had the best chance of disarming Kenny when the time came because he didn't really understand that she, too, had SWAT training. He thought she was just a paramedic.

She could feel Flint warning her to be patient, as if he, too, could feel the clock ticking. As wired as Kenny was, he would react badly to any attempt to disarm him in spite of the drugs he'd ingested. That short-barreled assault rifle could kill everyone in the room before Anna could get Kenny down. With luck, the drugs would slow his reflexes enough for her to get the upper hand.

Meanwhile there was Lee. Anna glanced over at him. He was standing by the door as if he knew not to get too close to the windows, his finger on the bomb switch, his gaze on Kenny. It seemed he was more worried about Kenny than anyone else in the room. At least for the moment.

More than ever, Anna knew it wouldn't take anything for Lee to go off, literally, and to take them all with him.

Anna waited, afraid what would happen next. She splayed her fingers on the floor in front of her, pretty sure Max had a clear view from the video camera in the vent. No. No. No. Do not breach.

"You plan to make a move when the pills do their job," Max said in her ear.

She smiled, signaled yes. She just prayed the pills would act quickly—but not too quickly. If Kenny thought she'd had something else put in them, he would shoot her.

She had no doubt of that as she met his gaze across the room.

CHAPTER ELEVEN

4:16 p.m.

FLINT WAITED, stealing a glance to where the tiny video and audio wires hung down from the air-conditioning vents, then he closed his eyes.

He wished he could try to get up, wished he was sure he would be able to when the time came. He was going on blind faith. In his heart he believed he could force his body to do whatever was needed to help save the people in this room. To save Anna, he believed he could perform miracles. At least, he hoped so.

He tried not to think about how dangerous it would be when the two of them made their move. He trusted Anna to handle her part.

With a wry smile, he realized that if anyone could pull this off, it would be Anna. Max had been right about that. She was remarkable. Flint still couldn't believe how she'd handled herself during all this. The woman had nerves of steel. She knew just what to say and do. If Gwendolyn Clark hadn't flipped out—

Anna laid a hand on his arm. Warm, soft, reassuring. He opened his eyes and smiled up at her. Her eyes said, *Not yet*. He'd seen that look five years ago, the night he'd finally gotten up the nerve to ask her to marry him.

They'd been on the Ferris wheel at the county fair after eating cotton candy and corn dogs and going on all the rides. Anna had known no fear. She'd wanted to ride everything, even the huge roller coaster.

That night he could deny her nothing. He won her a giant Panda bear, which they ended up giving to a little girl who'd been crying because she'd dropped her ice-cream cone. The little girl could have been theirs, with her big brown eyes and golden hair. Flint felt an ache like none he'd ever known for a family of his own.

As the night wound down, Anna wanted to go on just one more ride, the only one they'd missed. They climbed on the Ferris wheel, the basket rocking as it neared the top and the city lay before them, glittering like diamonds in the summer night. He looked over at Anna.

Kissing her was as natural as taking his next breath. He bent toward her, brushing his lips across hers. He heard her soft intake of breath and pulled back to look into her beautiful brown eyes. Then he cupped her face in his hands and kissed her with a passion he hadn't known he could feel. Anna surprised him with her own passionate response, giving as good as she got.

He could feel some of that reserve of hers evaporating, yet he still didn't know what she was so afraid of. Not him, he was sure of that. Marriage? He hoped not.

But as he took the ring out of his pocket, he felt her start to tremble. She was shaking her head, tears running down her cheeks. "Flint, no…"

He stuffed the ring box back into his pocket and took

her in his arms. "Talk to me, Anna. What is it? I know you're afraid. Is it me?"

She shook her head.

"What, then?"

"My sister."

"Emily?"

She shook her head. "Candace."

Candace? She had a sister named Candace? This was the first he'd heard about her. He thought about the photos he'd seen on the mantel at her house. No photo of a second sister. Frowning, he met her gaze.

"What happened to Candace?" he'd asked, knowing it had to be something so terrible that the family couldn't have her photographs around. Something so horrible that it kept Anna from trusting in his love for her....

Anna was looking down at him now, worry in her expression. She couldn't have been more beautiful. There was a radiance about her. He'd known from day one that she was special. That was one reason he'd wanted to make her his wife, the mother of his children.

Now, though, he realized just how selfish that had been. He'd wanted her all to himself. And when she'd talked about becoming a SWAT paramedic, he had been terrified he might lose her. And because of that, he *had* lost her.

"Flint?" she whispered, and cupped his cheek in her warm palm. "Are you sure you're all right?"

His eyes burned with regret. "I'm sorry, Anna," he whispered. "I was so wrong five years ago."

"Stop whispering over there," Kenny snapped.

"I'm just fixing his bandage," Anna said over her shoulder.

"Just patch him up and then get over here," he ordered.

"We can't wait, Flint," she whispered as she pretended to work on his bandage.

He nodded. "Let's do this."

Anna stared down at him, surprised by the look she'd seen in his eyes earlier. But that look had been replaced by one of determination. "Are you sure you can move?"

He gave her one of his quirky smiles and flexed his legs, trying to hide his grimace of pain from her. "No problem." He gave another signal to Max, using Anna to shield the sign from Lee and Flint.

"What's taking so long?" Kenny demanded suddenly, standing over them.

At first Anna thought he was talking about her checking Flint's bandage, but then Kenny added, "They should have gotten the money by now. They're just stringing me along, aren't they."

"I'm sure they are doing everything you asked them to," she said.

"Yeah, right." Kenny glared down at Flint. "Like sending in some SWAT commander posing as a doctor. I should kill him right now."

"He was just trying to protect me," she said, shifting a little to put herself between Kenny and Flint. "You would have done the same thing for your sister."

Kenny was silent. The drugs had stilled the restlessness in him some and, she hoped, hopefully slowed his reaction time.

"I should check your bandage," she said, pushing herself to her feet. She felt Flint's fingertips brush her wrist as she rose. "Why don't you come over here where I can get more light?"

4:32 p.m.

SURPRISINGLY, Kenny did as she told him. It was the calm in her voice, Flint thought. No matter what Kenny said or did, Anna just didn't get rattled. At least not on the surface. Flint had seen how she'd been trying to hold it together when he'd been wounded. She'd been scared that Kenny would kill him. Did he dare hope that there was a chance for them once this was over?

Max was right, Flint acknowledged once again as he watched Anna lead Kenny over to the window and realized what she was up to. Anna was damned good at this. Better than him. He let his emotions get in the way. He couldn't make that mistake again. Anna could teach him a thing or two about control and courage.

He watched her talk Kenny into opening the blind so she could inspect his injury and put a new bandage on it.

She was setting him up for a sharpshooter to take him out. Then it would be a matter of talking Lee down—if Lee didn't flip the switch at the first sound of gunfire.

Flint glanced over at the older man. Lee looked as lost as anyone Flint had ever seen.

"Lee," Flint said quietly, "could you hand me that?" He motioned to the second medical bag, the one Anna wasn't using. He had to get Lee closer, if he could. He also wanted another look at the bomb. If there was any chance he could diffuse it rather than have to take out Lee....

The timer on the bomb gave him hope that Lee had

programmed in a few minutes at least before the bomb blew up if Lee flipped the switch. *When* Lee flipped the switch.

Flint held no hope that he would be able to talk Lee out of it. He'd watched the older man deteriorate in front of his eyes all day, becoming more vague, seemingly more distant. It was clear that Lee had hoped no one would get hurt, but he seemed beyond that now.

Lee seemed to be in a daze, and it took him a moment to respond. Flint hated to think where the elderly man's thoughts had been as Lee bent awkwardly to pick up the bag from the floor and carry it over in his free hand. He set it beside Flint, his expression confused.

"I'm all right," Flint said, trying to comfort him—and also keep him close. "We're going to get these people out unharmed."

Lee's expression didn't change, but his gaze flickered to Flint's, and in that instant, Flint saw something that froze his blood. Lee Harper had already accepted that none of them would leave this room alive and that their blood would be on his hands for eternity.

Flint looked away, not wanting the man to see just how hard he planned to fight to keep that from happening. He'd gotten another good look at the bomb. The moment the marksman took Kenny out....

4:37 p.m.

"WE CAN'T GET a clear shot," Anna heard Max say into her earpiece.

She tried not to let her disappointment show and she

looked over at Flint. She had gotten Kenny by the window, opened the blind. Even if the shot missed, she was ready to take Kenny down. He'd ingested the drugs, his reflexes had to be slower. Flint had even managed to get Lee close to him.

She fought the tears of frustration and fear. The hours in this room were taking their toll. But it was Flint she was worried about. She needed to get him medical assistance. She needed to get these people out of here.

Kenny put down the blind again, moving away from the window, just as Lee was now moving away from Flint. The look on Flint's face echoed her own disappointment. They were on their own now. They would have to make another opportunity. Meanwhile, the drug she'd given Gwendolyn was wearing off and Lee wasn't looking good.

Max needed to reassure Kenny and soon. He needed to reassure them all.

Anna felt sick as she went over to Flint. He'd lost blood and should be taken to a hospital, yet Anna knew that trying to talk Kenny into letting Flint leave would be a waste of breath and only make matters worse. Not only that, Flint was their only chance of disposing of the bomb.

The phone rang. Kenny picked it up. "I'm tired of waiting." He was no longer yelling, and the quiet tone of his voice was more frightening. He listened. "Well, that's not quick enough. No, you can't have a hostage." He glanced at his watch. "If I don't have some proof that you're doing what I want, I'm going to kill one person every fifteen minutes. You got fifteen minutes." He slammed down the phone.

4:42 p.m.

FLINT SAW THE LOOK on Anna's face and knew, even before she came over to whisper to him, that Max was calling for a full breach in five minutes. She checked his bandage and he saw her fingers tremble.

Five minutes. Flint reached up, his fingers trailing down the side of her neck until he found her pulse.

It was strong, just like Anna. He had seen her disappointment, as acute as his own, when the sharpshooters hadn't taken a shot at Kenny. Flint wanted desperately to get her out of here.

He looked up at her, wanting to memorize the exact color of her eyes. He'd remembered them as being golden brown. But he saw now that there were spikes of gold—like flames—in the honey-brown.

Her pulse quickened under his fingertips, her flesh warm to the touch. He used to go down to the beach to watch her surf, awed by her talent. God, she was beautiful. All California girl. Her skin lightly browned by the sun and smooth, smelling of tanning oil and the Pacific.

She'd come out of the surf, saltwater beading on her tanned limbs, the surfboard under one arm, contentment softening her face.

It was that image that he thought about now; Anna silhouetted against the Pacific as the sun dipped slowly into the horizon.

"Lee will flip the switch," he whispered. "I'm not sure how much time we'll have." Flint was staking their lives on having a few minutes to get Lee to the window and out. He hated that that was his only choice. He would rather have tried to disarm the bomb.

He refused to believe that would be all the time they would have left together. Fate couldn't be so cruel to let Anna come back into his life, only to have him lose her. He prayed he would have a chance to get her back.

The words seemed to stick in his throat. "You'll have to keep Kenny busy."

"I'll do whatever it takes."

He smiled at that. His motto. At least it *had* been his motto. He felt as if everything had changed now. He'd changed. He didn't know who he would be if he ever got out of this room, out of this building. But he knew he wouldn't be the same man who'd come into it.

KENNY LEANED AGAINST the wall, pretending to drift with the drugs, all the time watching the two opposite him. The cops.

He was not a happy camper. The only thing he'd gotten that he'd asked for was the pills. The video camera had been Lee's dumb idea. How would they even know if his stupid statement aired? It wasn't like they had a TV. If Lee was so smart, why hadn't he thought to bring in a TV set? And some food?

Kenny had let Lee take Gwendolyn to the bathroom just off the meeting room. Lee had made her leave the door partway open and now Kenny had to listen to her whine. He should have just let her pee her pants. Would have served her right.

Kenny's stomach growled. He hadn't eaten since that

fast-food breakfast burrito this morning on the way here. What he wouldn't give for a cola. Hell, a beer.

He smiled at the memory of Lee sitting in the passenger seat of Kenny's car at the fast-food place. Lee hadn't wanted anything to eat. He'd wanted to take his own car, but Kenny had insisted they go together. If he'd known the guy had a bomb strapped to him, he would have let Lee have his own way and go alone.

Now Kenny wished he'd thought to at least bring a candy bar. What had made him think the city would get the money and the plane and passport before lunchtime? Bureaucracy never moved fast, he knew that, but he also knew they were stalling him, thinking they could outwait him. As if he had someplace to go, something to do besides sit here.

But he didn't like the way the two cops kept whispering to each other. He'd thought about separating them. Even thought about cuffing them instead of the hostages.

It seemed like more trouble than it was worth, though, and he couldn't trust Lee to do it anyway. Lee had screwed up everything he'd touched. Kenny wished the old fart would take his finger off that bomb switch. But even then, Kenny knew he'd be afraid to off the guy for fear the bomb would blow. Wasn't that what his sister would have called irony?

But as he watched the two cops, Kenny had an idea, one that gained appeal the more he thought about it. He liked the woman. He intended to keep her here until the end. But the guy cop he could live without, and it was time to send a message to the city. Forget waiting fifteen minutes. He needed to let the world outside this room know he was tired of waiting and wasn't taking it anymore.

"YOU'VE MADE ME a believer," Flint whispered to Anna, his gaze caressing her face. "You are definitely good at this. Better than me." He'd always been on the outside, giving orders, busting down doors, dropping in from helicopters. The easy part.

He realized he'd been dead wrong about what was right for her. He'd wanted to make this perfect little life with Anna at the center. He'd wanted to limit her possibilities to fit what he saw as her role not only in his life, but in the world around her.

"I was wrong, Anna," he whispered. "You're great at this. Much better than me."

She smiled as if she knew how hard it was for him to admit that.

"I was one selfish bastard," he whispered. "I was so damned wrong." He looked past her. Kenny was standing against the far wall, looking almost as lost as Lee. The pills had obviously taken effect or Flint figured he'd have been dead by now. He owed Anna his life. He just hoped the drugs would slow Kenny when Anna made her move.

The clock was running down. It was going to be time soon. Lee was still standing by the door like a sentry, but he didn't seem to be paying any attention to them. Flint knew he could be wrong on both counts.

He looked at Anna again. "I'm sorry," he whispered.

She met his gaze and nodded. He saw her swallow,

and tears glistened in her eyes before she looked away. This wasn't the time, he knew that. But he feared there might never be a time.

"I never stopped loving you."

She didn't look at him. She swallowed again and bit down on her lower lip.

There was a thud overhead. "What the hell?" Flint heard Kenny say.

Flint looked away from Anna, afraid of what he would see.

Kenny was staring up at the ceiling, cold fury in his eyes.

Flint followed his gaze to the wire the SWAT team had installed for audio and visual.

CHAPTER TWELVE

4:45 p.m.

"WHAT THE HELL?" Kenny cried again, shoving the pistol into a stunned Lee's free hand. "Anyone moves, shoot 'em."

Lee took the gun and pointed it at Flint, suspicion in his gaze, as well as confusion and fear.

Kenny dragged a chair over, climbed up and grabbed the wire, jerking it hard. It disconnected from the equipment and came snapping down like a whip. He had already spotted the other one and was sliding the chair across the floor toward it.

Anna heard Max swear softly in her ear as Kenny grabbed the second wire and jerked it free. He hurled it in the direction of the hostages, then jumped down, the veins in his neck bulging as he cursed the city and the cops and the sons of bitches who thought they could fool with him.

Gwendolyn was shrieking again, demanding that something be done in a voice that was only slightly slurred now that the drugs were wearing off.

Flint had pulled himself up against the wall. Anna could see that he was in terrible pain but she knew that he was getting ready for what was to come—all hell breaking loose. She was to take out Kenny, but he was raging again and expecting trouble.

The phone rang.

"That is going to cost you!" he screamed into the phone. "You hear me? You want to listen? Well, listen to this." He set down the phone, grabbed up the assault rifle and emptied a clip into the vent covers, sending a shower of debris down on them.

Before anyone could move, Kenny stepped to Flint and slammed the butt of the rifle into his head. Anna saw Flint fall over as Kenny grabbed her and dragged her to her feet. She struggled to free herself, to get to Flint, but Kenny had his arm around her neck and was cutting off her air as he pulled her away.

She couldn't see Flint, couldn't see if he was all right. Lee had moved and was now standing over him.

"You killed a cop," Lee said, his words like a blade to her heart.

"No!" Anna cried, trying to get to Flint, but Kenny only tightened his hold.

Past Lee, she caught a glimpse of Flint sprawled on the floor, unmoving. She began to cry, unable to hold back the tears, all her wonderful cool gone.

"Drag him out into the hall," Kenny ordered Lee. "Hurry. They want a hostage, they can have this one."

Anna fought to free herself of Kenny's hold, but he was strong, and with each struggle he only cut off more of her air. Black dots danced in front of her eyes and she could feel the pistol barrel pressing into her side. Why didn't he just kill her and get it over with?

Lee took his finger off the bomb switch and grabbed Flint's legs as Kenny half carried, half dragged her over to the door. Kenny shoved the desk aside and waited for Lee to pull Flint closer before he opened the door, staying back so he couldn't be seen from the hallway. So the SWAT team outside couldn't get a shot.

Flint couldn't be dead, Anna thought. Not after everything they'd been through. It wasn't over. It couldn't be. Flint was faking it, waiting for an opportunity. Lee had finally taken his finger off the bomb switch. Flint could stop him now.

Lee dragged Flint out into the hall and quickly put his finger back on the switch. Anna caught only a glimpse of Flint's body as Lee closed the door—just enough to see the lack of color in his face, not long enough to see if his chest rose and fell.

But she knew he wasn't faking it. If he had been, he would have overpowered Lee. He would have ended this.

And she was helpless to do anything. Kenny was slowly choking the life out of her. She could feel her will to live slipping away with it.

As Lee shoved the barricade back in front of the door, she quit fighting Kenny, all the fight gone out of her. Her knees buckled and Kenny let her sink to the floor at his feet.

"Anna?" Max said into her earpiece.

The phone rang. Kenny picked it up. "That's one. I'll kill another one in fifteen minutes," he said, and slammed down the receiver.

5:09 p.m.

BLADES OF AFTERNOON light sliced in through the blinds and flickered across the floor as a police helicopter thrummed past outside.

Anna looked across the room. Her eyes felt as if they were filled with sand. Grief and exhaustion made her limbs numb. She tried not to think how many hours she'd been in this room or how little time she had left on earth.

Kenny had been watching her from under hooded eyes. She knew who his next victim would be. A heavy silence had filled the room. The hostages were quiet. Even Gwendolyn. Kenny had said he would kill another hostage in fifteen minutes. Anna saw him look at his watch, then at her. It must be getting close to the time.

She closed her eyes and fought the image of Flint's lifeless body being dragged out of the room. She couldn't bear the thought that he was gone. That she would never see him again. It filled her with an emptiness that consumed her.

Lee shifted his position by the door. She glanced over at him, surprised at her own disinterest. Was this what happened to hostages after hours under constant threat of death? They became listless, the fear having drained them until they just wanted it over.

Lee looked as tired and lost as she felt. Why didn't he flip the switch? Or did he even remember why he had his finger on it? Anna wondered why Max hadn't gone full breach. She'd expected it as soon as the SWAT team found Flint's body.

She looked into Lee's dark eyes, idly wondering what

he was waiting for. Max had called to say Lee's video was running on all the five o'clock news stations in town. Kenny said he didn't give a damn.

Kenny knew he wasn't going to be getting any money or a plane and passport. He was angry, bitter that the movies and TV shows lied. She watched him glance at his watch, counting down the minutes, daring the SWAT team to come and get him.

Lee shifted again. He must know what Kenny had in mind. Would he try to stop Kenny from killing her? She wondered with the same disinterest that she felt about the bomb going off.

FLINT OPENED HIS EYES and knew right away that if he was dead, he hadn't made it to heaven. Not if T.C. Waters was here. He stared into the older cop's face for a moment, then tried to sit up.

T.C. pushed him back down. "Take it easy. You're in no shape to be moving. I've called for a stretcher."

Flint looked around, not surprised to see that he was in one of the rooms on the second floor of city hall. "Anna?"

T.C. shook his head.

"Max went full breach?" Flint asked, pushing T.C. back and sitting up. For a moment everything went dark, and he had to put his head down to keep from passing out.

"Max is holding, waiting for an update," T.C. said. "We're just minutes from full breach. You got one hell of a knot on your head and you're bleeding like a stuck pig."

"Give me your radio," Flint demanded. He hit the talk key. "Max, it's Flint. Hold your positions!"

"What's your status?" Max asked.

Flint knew he was asking about his medical condition as well as about Anna. Flint wished he knew. By now Kenny could have killed her. There was no doubt in Flint's mind that Anna would be next.

"I'm going back in," Flint said. "I'm going to need a few minutes inside before you come in."

"Negative. T.C. reported that you're wounded."

"T.C. exaggerates. I'm fine. I'm going back in. I can do this."

"Put T.C. on," Max said.

T.C. was shaking his head.

Then Flint heard Max ask, "T.C., is he up to it?"

Flint shot T.C. a look.

T.C. took the radio Flint handed him. "You know Flint," T.C. said, his gaze locked with Flint's.

"Answer the question," Max snapped.

"I'd put my life in his hands," T.C. said.

Flint managed a smile. "Just patch me up and get me a weapon," he told T.C.

Flint didn't need T.C. to tell him that he wouldn't be on his feet long. He didn't need T.C. to tell him that he'd lost a lot of blood and that he wasn't as strong as he probably thought he was. T.C. was smart enough not to tell him anything as he helped Flint up.

The radio squawked. "Flint?"

"Here," Flint said into the radio. "I'm ready to roll, Max."

"I'll stall Kenny. You've got two minutes once you're inside."

Two minutes. He knew what he had to do. Take out the bomb, one way or another. He couldn't be sure that

Anna would be able to help him. He pushed away the thought. Somehow he'd get her out along with the rest of the hostages. "Two minutes," he said into the radio.

Gritting his teeth to hide his pain, he looked up for a vent. He felt woozy and his side hurt like hell. But his body wouldn't let him down. It couldn't, not now. "Can you connect me with Anna so I can tell her the plan?"

"Yes," Max answered. He didn't have to say, If she still has her earpiece. If she's still alive.

"Then let's rock and roll," Flint said, turning to T.C. "Show me which vent I need to take." There were a half dozen men in position to storm the meeting room. "Full breach two minutes after I drop into the room."

T.C. exchanged a look with the other team members, then said to Flint, "This way, boss."

Flint gave his men a nod. He couldn't have hand-picked a better bunch for the job.

As he and T.C. reached the entrance to the air-conditioning vent, Flint turned to him. "No matter what happens," Flint said quietly, "get Anna out if you can."

"She's the one who broke your heart, isn't she? The one you were engaged to."

"Yeah." Flint pulled up a chair, climbed up painfully and lifted the vent cover. The duct work was large enough for a man his size, but just barely. He stopped to catch his breath, hanging on to the opening, suddenly afraid he'd been wrong. Maybe he couldn't do this. Maybe his body would let him down.

"She dumped you," T.C. said below him.

"Yeah."

"So what's changed?"

"I have," Flint said, and wasn't surprised when T.C. was suddenly beside him on a chair, helping him into the duct. Without looking back, Flint began to crawl quietly into the darkness.

FLINT HAD BEEN DATING Anna for almost six months when she'd finally confided in him about Candace.

They'd gone for a walk after dinner at one of the small fishing shack cafés. Anna had been unusually quiet all night. In his pocket was the engagement ring in the small velvet box he'd been carrying around for months.

But that night he had the awful feeling that she was going to break up with him. The warm night air smelled of salt and fish. He'd come to love Southern California. Anna had taught him to bodysurf. He loved the sea and Anna. In his mind they would always be linked.

"Candace was my older sister," Anna told him, as if the words were a stone that had been lodged in her throat. "She was murdered."

He stopped and, taking her arm, turned her to face him. "Anna, I'm so sorry."

She bit her lower lip. "She was killed by her fiancé."

He stared at Anna, suddenly understanding her reluctance to date, let alone trust a man.

"We all loved him." She was crying, the words tumbling out. "He was funny and fun. He was like a big brother. He used to take me and Emily along on some of their dates and he would buy us ice-cream cones. He was so…perfect. He was family."

Flint could only shake his head.

"We didn't know. He fooled us all. Except Candace." Anna's voice broke as she choked back a sob. "She had put off the wedding. We were angry with her and questioning what was wrong with *her.* She knew she shouldn't be marrying him. But she never said anything. Probably because we wouldn't have believed her. Even when we saw the bruises, we didn't suspect anything. Darrel said love had made her uncoordinated and joked that he hoped their kids inherited his genes."

Flint looked away, the sea wallowing restlessly in the horizon. "She tried to break it off," he said, knowing that was the case even before he looked over at her again. Waves lapped at their feet, but neither of them seemed to feel the cool water.

"He said he would rather see her dead than with anyone else," Anna told him.

"What happened to him?" Flint asked.

"He turned the gun on himself after he shot her."

Flint had squeezed her hand, finally understanding why she'd been so scared of falling for a man. With his other hand, he'd cupped the back of her head and gently pulled her to him. He'd cradled her in his arms, the surf foaming around their ankles, the lights coming on down the beach as the warm darkness settled in around them.

5:16 p.m.

THE PHONE RANG, startling everyone in the room. Kenny dropped the rifle. It clattered to the floor, and it took him a few moments to pick it up. The drugs *had* slowed his reflexes, Anna thought. He'd taken a couple more of the pills, breaking the container to get them out rather than ask her to open the cap for him again.

He glanced at his watch now as the phone rang again, then blinked and picked up the receiver.

"The video Lee Harper made aired," she heard Max say to Kenny via her earpiece. "The governor called me. He's authorized me to make a deal."

She saw hope shine in Kenny's glazed eyes for a moment, then quickly die.

"This is another stall, isn't it," Kenny snapped.

"I'm going to have you out of there within the half hour," Max said. "You have my word. But only if you don't hurt anyone else."

In answer, Kenny swung the assault rifle in an arc and pulled the trigger. Anna dove for cover as bullets riddled the wall behind her. Plaster showered down on her and the hostages. Her ears rang from the noise, and then there was an eerie silence.

She waited for Max to say something.

Silence in her earpiece.

Kenny hung up the phone. "I think he's finally realized I mean business."

Anna knew that Max hadn't meant that Kenny would be leaving on a jet plane. Within the hour, Max would have them all out, one way or another. The SWAT team would be coming in soon. All hell was about to break loose. Max had been trying to warn her.

What about Flint? Why hadn't Max said something about Flint? Because he was dead.

She stared at the bullet-riddled wall over the hostages, then at Kenny, anger shaking off her earlier numbing despair. She wanted to be the one who took down Kenny. He'd killed Flint. She felt her blood coursing through her extremities again. With it came a heart-wrenching pain, but also a calculated fury.

"We're coming in. Be ready for the phone call," Max said in her ear.

She was ready.

5:19 p.m.

THE AFTERNOON SUN dappled the floor of the city hall meeting room. Kenny stared at it, the assault rifle across his lap, the pistol within reach.

The drugs were working. He could feel the mellow along with the melancholy that often came with it. He felt defeated, but then he'd felt that way much of his life.

As he looked across the ransacked room, blood on the floor, a dull constant ache in his arm, he told himself he wasn't going to be getting money or a plane or a passport to some safe foreign country. The bastards had lied.

The kicker was, he didn't want to go to some foreign country anyway. With his luck, people there wouldn't speak English. He'd have to learn some damned foreign language, and what would he do once the money and pills ran out?

He glanced over at Lee. What a crazy bastard. This was all his fault. Him and his stupid ideas. Kenny wished to hell he hadn't gotten involved with the old fool. His life would have been a hell of a lot better if he'd never met Lee, never heard his hard-luck story. Kenny had enough hard-luck stories of his own.

He wished he were in that dinky drab apartment he was about to be kicked out of. At least he still had cable TV, and there were a couple of beers in the fridge. He could be watching "Wheel of Fortune" right now, his feet up in his ragged recliner.

Under the fluorescent light inside the meeting room, he watched the nurse-cop get up and come toward him. He told himself maybe under other circumstances he might have asked her for a date. He doubted she would have said yes, but *maybe* she would have gone out with him. No chance of that now. He was going to kill her in a few minutes.

"How's your arm?" she asked, coming to stand directly in front of him.

He motioned her back with the rifle.

"Your bandage needs changing," she said.

He shook his head. At the back of his mind he was considering who he'd kill after her. He'd save the judge for last, but eventually he'd kill them all, and then Lee would blow them both to hell—if he didn't do it sooner.

The idea of going out in a blaze of glory rather than with his hands up had some appeal. Kenny wasn't wild about jail. He'd been there before. Prison wasn't too bad. They at least had HBO and you got fed.

"It looks like your arm's bleeding again," she said. "You need to stay still."

Maybe he would just bleed to death right here. That's where the cops would find him. Dead against this wall.

No, that would be worse than prison.

"Leave me alone." He pointed the barrel of the gun at her, his words slurred. The drugs had knocked him on his ass. He wanted to blame the nurse, but she'd told him not to take so many.

She knelt beside him and he remembered how she'd opened the child-proof cap on his drugs. His eyes smarted with tears. Hers had been the only kindness he'd had since his sister died. She began to undo his bandage. He was going to hate to have to kill her.

LEE BLINKED and looked around, surprised to find himself still standing in some room. He didn't know where. He didn't know how long he'd been standing here. He didn't seem to be wearing his watch.

As he looked down at his wrist, he saw the device taped to his chest and frowned, his finger twitching, his body going cold as he remembered getting on the Internet, searching for bombs.

Francine. She was gone. That's why he was here. That's why these people were here, he thought as he looked around the room, saw their fear, felt his own.

Francine. He missed the way they used to make cookies together. He was always in charge of cutting up the nuts for the oatmeal cookies he loved.

They used to joke that they had assisted living. He assisted her and she assisted him.

He remembered her crying and frowned. They'd been to see his doctor and gotten the bad news. Alzheimer's. The doctor said he had Alzheimer's and was losing his mind.

Tears blurred his vision. Francine had told him not to worry. She'd take care of him. But Francine was gone, her death an ache he would no longer endure. He knew she was waiting for him on the other side. So what was he doing standing in this room? He could no longer remember. He could no longer wait. It was time he joined his wife.

KENNY STILL HAD the assault rifle resting on his lap, but he'd pulled out the pistol and was holding it in his free hand, the barrel pointed at her chest.

He wasn't as out of it as Anna had hoped. "Leave the damned bandage alone," he snapped, motioning her away with the pistol.

The hostages had been silent as death. But now she heard the rustle of clothing. Like her, they knew something was about to happen. They just didn't know what.

Anna looked into Kenny's eyes, wondering what he was thinking.

"Get back."

Something in his tone made her rise to her feet and step back slowly. She glanced at the hostages. Gwendolyn's eyes were wide as saucers, her face tear-streaked. She was staring at Kenny, no doubt hoping he wouldn't change his mind about who to kill next.

Kenny got to his feet. It must be time. She stopped and estimated the distance between them and the best way to get the assault rifle and pistol away from him.

He glanced at his watch, then quickly back to her as he raised the barrel of the rifle a little higher, taking aim.

The phone rang. Kenny froze. It didn't ring a second time. He looked down at the phone lying on the floor, then back up at her. Did he realize it was a signal?

"Anna," came the soft whisper in her ear, the familiar voice sending goose bumps over her skin. Flint.

Tears sprang to her eyes and she had to close them for fear Kenny would see and know. Relief made her weak. Flint was alive! No matter what happened in this room, Flint was alive.

"Baby," Flint said, his voice breaking.

I'm here, she wanted desperately to answer. *I'm here, Flint.*

"Get ready. I'm coming in the vent near Kenny."

She opened her eyes.

Kenny was smiling ruefully. "It's time. Turn around."

"I love you," Flint said.

She blinked back tears and looked Kenny in the eye. "Yes," she agreed. "It's time."

The vent behind Kenny banged down in a thunder of noise and dust as Flint Mauro dropped into the room.

FLINT HIT THE FLOOR hard, the jarring drop knocking the wind out of him. Pain shot through him and his side was on fire, his vision blurring for an instant. He didn't need to look to know that he'd started the wound bleeding again.

He shot a glance in Anna's direction. She was already moving, flying at Kenny.

Flint didn't have the time to wait to see if she would succeed. His gaze leaped to Lee.

"You don't want to do that," Flint said quietly, shaking his head as he moved swiftly toward the older man, keeping the trauma scissors in his hand hidden. "Let these people walk away now. You don't want any more blood on your hands."

Lee stumbled back. Flint heard a grunt come out of Kenny, then a loud thud as he hit the floor.

There was that instant when Lee had looked relieved to see Flint alive, relieved that this day would finally be over. But clearly Lee was determined not to leave this room alive.

As Lee flipped the switch, Flint launched himself at the older man—and the bomb.

CHAPTER THIRTEEN

As LEE REMOVED his finger from the bomb, he looked at Flint, regret as well as resolve evident in his expression. Lee closed his eyes, waiting for the inevitable. A small hand on the watch began to tick off the seconds.

Flint thought it was funny what came to a person's mind at a moment like this. Bomb squad guys had jokes for such times. "You have the rest of our life to dismantle this bomb" or "Your only mistake will be your last."

Grabbing Lee, Flint shoved him back against the door and looked down at the bomb. He could feel sweat drip off his forehead as he produced the trauma scissors and cut through the duct tape that held the bomb to the elderly man.

The pain in his side was making him nauseous, the pain in his head blurring his vision. He ripped the blades down through the tape on one side and then the other, feeling the seconds ticking by. He was still on his feet. That was about all he could say.

Flint knew his orders. Get Lee out a window. But the windows were on the far wall and he'd have to get the man over there. He had to throw him out and pray that Lee dropped far enough before the bomb went off so the hostages handcuffed to the radiators by the window weren't injured.

There was a second option—one Max wouldn't have approved. He could free Lee and get rid of the bomb.

Timing was everything, Flint thought, and wanted to laugh. He tried not to think about Anna, or what was happening behind him. Or that any moment he might feel a bullet from Kenny's weapon rip through him.

He had two minutes from the time he hit the floor to when the rest of the SWAT team came into this room.

The duct tape cut, he started to peel the bomb off the old man, a little surprised Lee made no effort to stop him. Instead the elderly man seemed to be watching, as if he were a spectator, interested in what Flint would do next.

That's when Flint saw that Lee had put in a fail-safe mechanism. If Flint removed the bomb, it would blow instantly.

ANNA GRABBED Kenny's wounded arm and twisted. He had already proven how strong he was. And she knew he would be fighting to the death.

He let out a cry. The assault rifle clattered to the floor, but as she started to go for it, he backhanded her with his good arm and sent her sprawling.

She kicked out, striking him in the face, then lunged toward the rifle. He already had his hands on it and was trying to swing it around to fire at her.

She struggled with him, kicking at his body, connecting with his shoulder, making him howl in pain as he fell backward, hitting hard on the floor.

Behind her, she knew Flint was trying to disarm the bomb. She refused to let herself think that at any moment they could all be blown to smithereens. She wanted to get Kenny. He had hurt Flint, almost killed him. Still might. She couldn't let Kenny get the rifle, no matter what she had to do.

She swung an elbow into his face and felt his nose break, heard him squeal. His fingers on the rifle loosened just enough that she got better purchase. She jerked it away from him, rolled and swung it around, pointing the barrel end at Kenny. "Don't give me an excuse to kill you," she yelled.

He stared at her. "Some Florence friggin' Nightingale you are."

FLINT'S GAZE FLEW to Lee's. The older man was looking right at him, a smug, satisfied expression on his face.

Swearing, Flint glanced down at the timer. Seven seconds had gone by.

He jerked the man off his feet and felt pain sear up his side. The window. He had to get Lee to the window, but his arms felt like lead and the dark spots were back dancing in front of his eyes. He saw Anna on the floor with the gun. Kenny on his hands and knees.

Flint pulled Lee toward the windows, feeling as if his feet were running in slow motion. He hadn't been expecting Lee to punch him in his wounded side. He felt the air rush from his lungs as he doubled over, losing his grip on Lee.

Before Flint could react, Lee broke loose and ran toward the windows. He was fairly spry for his age. Or maybe like Flint, the old man had willed his body to perform out of necessity one last time.

Flint watched as Lee launched himself, dipped a shoulder to take the brunt of the panes and dove through the shattering window.

Glass and bits of wood sprayed the hostages.

For an instant Flint saw Lee Harper silhouetted against the afternoon light.

Then the man dropped, disappearing from sight.

Flint stared after him for only an instant before he hurled himself at Anna to shield her body from the explosion.

At the impact of falling on her, a blanket of darkness dropped over him. He didn't hear the explosion, feel the debris that fell from the ceiling or smell Anna's scent as she cupped his face, her tears falling on his cheek, and cradled him in her arms.

Like Lee, Flint was in his own world now, far from the pain of this one.

FOR ANNA, everything was a blur. The SWAT team had come into the room, taking Kenny Reese down just before the bomb exploded outside.

It had been her voice saying, "The keys to the handcuffs are in Kenny's pocket." She remembered someone crying. It could have been her. She thought she recalled Councilwoman Gwendolyn Clark threatening to sue the city.

She'd helped get Flint on a stretcher and rode in the ambulance to the hospital, but the image that stayed in her mind was of him dropping down through that vent. Her hero. Flint, strong, courageous. Flint, vividly alive.

At the hospital, the emergency staff had taken Flint to surgery and had patched up her cuts and scrapes. Max had driven her home to her apartment.

That night she slept on the deck. She couldn't stand being inside. She had wanted to stay at the hospital with Flint, but Max had ordered her to go home.

She waited for his call, afraid when the phone finally rang.

"Flint's out of surgery and in recovery," Max said. "He just needs rest now. There is nothing more you can do. Get some sleep. You've been through a hell of a first day of work."

Out on the deck, she sprawled on her back, staring up at the stars, listening to the ocean. It had never sounded so sad to her before. The stars blurred. She hadn't really let herself cry yet. She'd passed exhaustion hours ago. Now she felt jittery, as if her nervous system had been amped up and she might blow a fuse at any moment. She closed her eyes, but the darkness seemed worse.

She stared up at the stars again, trying to find one to wish on. It had to be the right star. She made her wish. Flint was going to be all right. He had to be. The surgery had gone well, Max had told her. And Flint was strong.

Tears blurred the stars overhead as she thought about him saving her life tonight. He'd come back for her. Alone.

He could have been killed. They all could have been killed, but Flint had saved her. Saved Kenny and the hostages. Lorna was in the hospital. Her surgery had gone well, too. She was expected to make it.

Only Lee had been lost. She felt a deep sense of sorrow for the tormented man. He was with Francine now. That was all he'd really wanted.

Flint had tried so hard to save him, but sometimes saving another human being was impossible. Some people didn't want to be saved.

She must have slept because the phone startled her eyes open. The sun was up, casting her view of the ocean in gold.

She went into the apartment and caught the phone on the fourth ring.

"Anna, it's Dad."

Taking a deep breath, Anna sank down onto the edge of the bed, overwhelmed at just the sound of his voice and surprised to find she was crying.

"Honey, I heard what happened. Are you all right?"

She couldn't speak. The sobs hurt her throat and her eyes ran with tears.

"Anna?"

"I'm all right."

"I'm calling you from the Sacramento airport. I'll be in Courage Bay in two hours. Can you pick me up at the airport there?"

She was so relieved that he was coming. "I'll be there. Dad?"

"Yes?"

"Thank you."

"See you soon, honey."

When she'd hung up, she looked around the apartment, spotting Flint's old faded T-shirt in the wastebasket where she'd thrown it—when was that? It seemed like another lifetime ago.

She pushed herself up and walked over to the waste-basket. She'd been so sure she was over Flint. Slowly she reached down and picked up the T-shirt, bringing the soft, worn cloth to her face, breathing in the remembered scent of him. Crushing the shirt to her chest, she called the hospital. Flint's T-shirt was clutched in one hand when she was told that he'd survived the night. She hung up and sobbed in relief into the cloth.

A while later she went to shower and change clothes. She had to see Flint before she drove to pick up her father at the airport.

THE AIRPORT WAS BUSY as usual. She stood in the visitors area, watching for her father, wondering if he would recognize her, she felt so different.

He spotted her and waved, frowning a little as he came closer. Then he was through the door and she was in his arms.

She didn't break down until they reached her apartment. "Flint almost died," she said, crying again. She couldn't remember ever crying this much. Except when Candace had died. "Flint risked his life for me."

"Anna, Flint is the head of the SWAT team," her father argued. "He would have risked his life no matter what."

She shook her head. "This is all my fault. I'm the reason he joined SWAT. This isn't what he wanted. He did it because of me."

"Honey," her father said, taking both of her hands in his. "You can't take on responsibility for the whole world."

"That isn't what I'm doing."

"It's what you have always done, Anna. I watched you after your sister was killed. You seemed to think you could make everything right. I watched you try so hard to be Candace for your mother."

Tears welled in her eyes at the realization that it was true. Only she'd failed to replace the daughter her mother had lost and she'd seen that failure every day in her mother's eyes.

"What about what you want, Anna? If Candace was still alive, what would you be doing right now?"

She stared at him. "I don't know."

"You wouldn't be a paramedic on the SWAT team, would you?"

She got up and walked across the room.

"What do *you* want?" he asked. "What do you want right now?"

She turned to face him. "I want Flint to live. I want to get the chance to tell him how sorry I am."

Her father lifted a brow. "If you had only two minutes to talk to him, what would you really want to say to him."

She stared at her father. "I'd tell him that I still love him, that I doubt I ever stopped loving him."

Her dad nodded and smiled. "And?"

"And...I want to be with him."

"What about your job?"

She shook her head. "That's what broke us up before." She sat down heavily in one of the overstuffed chairs. "Nothing has changed and yet everything has changed. I've changed," she said, looking up at him. "I don't know what I want to do with my life anymore. I just know that I desperately want Flint in it."

"So you would give up your career for him? That must be horribly frightening to think you love him that much."

She smiled at her father. "It scares me half to death. Do you think I'm wrong to give up what I love for a man?"

"Do I think you're wrong to love a man that much?" He shook his head. "The question is, how much does he love you? Does he love you enough to let you make the decision about your job?"

"You don't think I should quit my job."

"I can't tell you what to do, Anna. But whatever it is, do it for the right reasons."

"Is that what you flew up here to tell me?"

He smiled. "I had to make sure you really were all right."

She nodded. "I am. But I feel like I've been given another chance. I just don't know to do what."

"Don't you?" her father asked with a smile.

FLINT OPENED HIS EYES. At first he didn't see her with the sun streaming into the hospital room. She was sitting in a chair by the window, her hair glowing golden in the sun, her head down as if she had been here for some time, waiting.

He didn't move, didn't dare breathe for fear she might be a mirage and, if he blinked, she would be gone. He'd been dreaming about her. In the dream, she lived with him in a house with a view of the ocean from the patio, and palm trees and a pool.

He couldn't remember the wedding in the dream, but he was acutely aware of the gold band on the finger of his left hand and the way he woke up next to her each morning.

And of course they had kids. He could hear the little darlings coming down the hallway toward his and Anna's bedroom. The patter of tiny feet moving on a wave of giggles and bright morning sunshine. He smiled. He had waited in the dream for his and Anna's children to come through the open door of the bedroom with an expectation that was more like an ache.

But then he'd opened his eyes and seen that he was in a hospital room. The disappointment had been acute until he'd seen Anna sitting in the chair by the window. He'd felt a surge of hope so elusive that he'd held his breath, afraid to say anything to her for fear this, too, was only a dream.

"You're awake."

His heart swelled at the sound of her voice. She stepped out of the sunlight, no longer silhouetted against the window, her face coming into view. No mirage.

She reached to ring the nurse and he saw that her hands were shaking.

"Anna," he said, his mouth so dry it came out a whisper. He didn't take his eyes from her, afraid he might blink and she would be gone again. She had a bruise on her forehead and a small cut at the corner of her mouth. When she moved, he saw her favor one side as if it were sore or injured.

But she was all right. He could see that in her eyes. Her brown eyes, which filled with tears as she touched his hand. Just a brush of skin against skin, as if she were afraid to touch him, afraid she might hurt him.

They had survived. His heart swelled at the realization. And they'd done it against all odds. He felt choked up as he recalled how close they had come to not being here.

"The hostages?" he asked, his throat aching.

"They all got out. Lorna came through surgery. She's expected to make it. I heard that the other hostages have been coming by to visit her." Anna made a swipe at her tears. "She really was something under fire, wasn't she?"

"Like someone else I know," Flint said, and tried to sit up.

"Easy." She touched his shoulder. "The doctor said you're lucky to be alive. You lost a lot of blood and you have a concussion. You've been out of it for the last forty-eight hours."

He hadn't realized he'd been gone that long. It surprised him.

"You got hit so hard…"

He saw the tears glistening in her eyes again. He reached up to take her hand, awkwardly thumbing the inside of her palm, trying to find the words he needed to say.

"You were amazing," he said, looking into her eyes.

"You were the one who was amazing."

He shook his head, then stopped because it hurt too badly. He took a breath. He couldn't remember ever being this tired, this filled with emotion. He knew he needed to sleep, to get his strength back, to make sure he said the right words to her.

But his need to tell her how he felt outweighed everything else. "I was wrong about…everything."

She tried to hush him. "The doctor said you had to lie still and get rest."

The nurse came into the room and hurried to his bedside. "So you're awake," she said, and set about checking his vitals.

He kept his gaze on Anna, frustrated that he hadn't been able to say everything that was on his mind. He could feel exhaustion making his body heavy, his eyelids almost impossible to keep open.

The nurse turned to Anna. "He really needs his rest."

"No," Flint managed to say, but he felt her hand slip from his. He'd never been able to hang on to this woman. "I have to tell you—"

"All that matters is that you get better," she said. "Rest. We'll have plenty of time to talk later."

He fought to keep his eyes open. He could feel fatigue dragging him back under. But it wasn't the wounds that were causing him the pain. "I have to tell you, Anna," he whispered. He felt her lips brush his cheek. "I have to…"

As FLINT DRIFTED BACK to sleep, Anna stared down at his pale face and the bandage on his head, both in stark contrast to his black hair. Her heart swelled with relief that he had awakened. He had scared her so badly.

The doctors said that between the loss of blood, chance of infection and the concussion, Flint was very lucky to be alive. She'd stayed by his side most of the last forty-eight hours, fearing that he might not survive after everything he had done to save her and the lives of the hostages. It broke her heart, knowing he had tried to save Lee, as well.

She closed her eyes at the thought of Lee and what

had happened to him. Kenny had been taken into custody. He was facing a variety of charges that would put him back in prison for a very long time.

Gwendolyn Clark was suing the city. Her uncle, Judge Craven, had commended both Anna and Flint, saying they had done an outstanding job under the worst kind of conditions.

"You still here?" Max asked, peering in through the hospital room door.

"He woke up," she said, and heard her voice break. Tears welled in her eyes and she fought them back, not wanting to cry in front of her boss.

"You know how tough he is," Max said, joining her. "How could you doubt he wouldn't make it?"

She could hear the relief in his voice. He'd been afraid, too.

Max was shaking his head as he looked down at Flint. "He's a damned fool. He had no business going back into that room. Always has to be the Lone Ranger." Max smiled as he turned to her. Taking her arm, he led her out of the room. "You look as if you could use a little rest yourself. Did I mention that the two of you did a hell of a job?"

"We were just doing our jobs," she said.

Max made a rude sound. "Save that for the press. This is you and me, Anna. I should never have let the two of you go in there. I'm damned lucky you didn't all get killed. I would never have forgiven myself."

As they left Flint's room and walked through the hospital, suddenly she needed to see the ocean, hear the surf breaking on the sandy beach, smell the salt and feel the sun on her face. The hospital hallway seemed too narrow, too confining, too much like the meeting room at city hall.

"Are you all right?" Max asked.

She nodded. Flint was going to make it. Everything was all right. "I just need…rest," she managed to say.

Max nodded. "An experience like you've been through… Of course you need rest. Why don't you go home? I'll hang around here for when Flint wakes up again. It's over, Anna." He patted her shoulder.

Over. Until the next time.

Max seemed to read her thoughts. "Things will look different after you've had sufficient rest."

She wasn't so sure about that, but she nodded and walked out into the last of the day's sunshine, gulping the air, choking back tears as she headed toward the car, where her father was waiting for her.

"How is Flint?" he asked.

She brushed at her tears. "He woke up. That's a good sign. The doctor thinks he'll pull through as long as the wound doesn't get infected." She began to cry again. "I'm so scared, Dad."

"I know, honey. But you're both alive and both heroes."

She shook her head. She felt like anything but a hero.

"Anna, you should be proud of what you were able to accomplish. Flint couldn't have done it without you."

"Dad, I never understood why he didn't want me to be a part of SWAT until we started in there and I realized I might lose him."

He raised an eyebrow. "Lose him? Anna, you broke off the engagement five years ago."

She shook her head again. "It's all so complicated and confusing. I think I made a terrible mistake."

"Leaving Flint?" he asked.

Looking away, she took a breath and pulled herself together. "Maybe everything I've done was a mistake."

He laughed softly. "Anna, you've been so successful at everything you've attempted. How can you possibly say that?"

"Dad, I've been involved in hundreds of incidents, some more dangerous than others," she said, trying to put the feelings into words, trying desperately to understand it herself. "But when I was in city hall with Flint, trapped in that room, knowing we were probably going to die…" Her voice trailed off. "I'm not sure what happened. It just changed everything."

Her dad nodded. "Let me drive. There's someplace we need to go. Someplace you've put off going for years."

She stared over at him, afraid she knew where he was taking her. The last place on earth she wanted to go.

CHAPTER FOURTEEN

FLINT DRIFTED IN and out of consciousness. He couldn't tell what was real and what was a dream. Had Anna been here in his hospital room at one point? He couldn't be sure. Had he told her how he felt? He'd rehearsed the words in his head so much, maybe he only thought she'd been here and that he'd told her.

This time when he woke, the sun had set and the room was dim—and empty. No Anna. He felt desolate and tried to tell himself it was the drugs and the pain. But he knew it was the fear that Anna was gone from his life.

He closed his eyes and let himself drift. Memories washed through the drug-induced mist behind his eyelids.

He thought about Anna. About having a wife who was a paramedic on the SWAT team. He wouldn't deal with that now. He could think about happier times. He pictured her standing in the doorway, wearing that old T-shirt of his. She was smiling. Her laugh hung on the air, a wonderful, joyous sound.

Flint clung to that sound as he drifted off to sleep.

ANNA WALKED ACROSS the perfectly groomed lawn, her father at her side. The sun had sank behind the palms and now cast long shadows through the cemetery. She had cried so much, her throat was raw and her eyes felt scratchy and dry. She feared she had no more tears, as if her grief was a well that had finally run dry.

As she looked over at her dad, she realized how much she missed their weekly lunches. She felt she was losing everyone who mattered in her life and she couldn't bear it.

There had been too much change. Her parents' divorce. Their moves to other cities. Even Emily leaving for Seattle.

"Remember the day I told you that Flint had asked me to marry him?" she asked her dad softly as they walked.

He nodded. "I was surprised, and sorry you'd turned him down."

"You asked me why. You asked me if I loved him," she said.

"I remember." He stopped walking, and she knew without looking that they were almost to her sister's grave.

Tears burned her eyes. It was impossible to explain how she felt. Even to her dad. She'd promised herself she wouldn't cry, and yet her eyes blurred with tears. "I can't..."

He stepped to her, forcing her to look up at him. "Candace's death affected all of us in different ways. I don't have to tell you what it did to your mother. Emily was so young, it didn't have as much of an impact on her as it did on you."

"Dad—"

"I think you're trying to make up for what happened somehow," he said, sounding sad.

"I can't see how my becoming a paramedic has anything to do with what happened with Candace."

"Can't you? Isn't she the reason you were determined to join the SWAT team?"

Anna shook her head, more in frustration than anything else. "Even if it is—"

"Candace was killed by a man who had sworn to love her," her dad said. "Don't tell me you're not afraid that you might make the same mistake. It's why you turned down Flint's proposal the first time."

She looked away, surprised her father knew her so well. "Do you remember how much we all loved Darrel?" she asked. "He seemed so perfect, not just for Candace but for our family." She turned to look at him again. "I knew something was wrong toward the end. Candace wasn't happy. She tried to talk to me about it but I told her—" She choked back the tears.

"I told her it was just cold feet," she continued, needing to finally tell someone. "I loved Candace but I thought she was going to mess everything up. I didn't care if she was happy or not. I wanted her to marry Darrel. Darrel was family, he loved all of us…" Her voice broke. She'd loved Darrel, and maybe that was what hurt the most. Anna had loved Darrel like a brother, the brother she'd always wanted. "I never told anyone before what I said to Candace, how I encouraged her to marry Darrel when she didn't want to."

"We all loved Darrel." Her father lifted her chin so that their eyes met. "I was no different than you, Anna. I wanted Darrel in our family. Candace tried to talk to me once about the problems they were having." He looked away, swallowed. His eyes were shiny when he met her gaze again. "I told her every couple has problems."

Anna felt as if a weight had been lifted off her shoulder as she stepped into her dad's arms and he hugged her tightly.

"We have to quit blaming ourselves," he said, pulling back to wipe his eyes. "All of us."

Anna stared at him and saw something she had missed before. She'd been so caught up in her own guilt over Candace that she hadn't seen it before this moment. "You think Candace confided in Mother."

Her dad winced. "I think your mother is carrying more guilt than she's been able to handle for many years. Over Candace. Over you."

"Me?"

"I know your mother wishes she could go back and do things differently," he said.

She stepped back from the hug. Her dad had always made excuses for her mother. She looked past him toward the sea. It was her compass, she realized. She felt grounded when she had it as a place to start. The one thing she'd done right was to come back here. "Doesn't Flint seem too perfect to you?"

Her dad laughed. "No man is perfect, honey. There was something terribly wrong with Darrel, Anna, you know that. He was crazy jealous of Candace…."

"What if there is something terribly wrong with Flint?"

Her dad smiled and shook his head. "Anna, you have to trust your judgment. I trust it. You're in love with him. Listen to your heart."

"What if my heart is wrong?" she asked, her voice sounding close to tears. Just like Candace's heart had originally been. Anna could remember only too well when Candace was happy with Darrel, the way her whole face would light up when he walked into a room, or the way she smiled when she picked up the phone and it was him calling.

Anna remembered because she'd hoped that one day she would meet someone like Darrel. And she had met someone who made her feel airborne at just the sight of him, whose voice made her heart beat a little faster. She loved Flint and it scared her to death.

"Anna, you're a smart woman. I have a feeling you've already figured this out for yourself. Whatever happened in that room at city hall…" His gaze met hers and she saw the pain and worry. Her father didn't like her being in this dangerous job any more than Flint. The difference was, he hadn't tried to stop her.

She hugged him again.

"Are you all right?" he asked, pulling back to look at her.

She smiled through her tears. "Maybe I went into this for all the wrong reasons, but I'm good at it, Dad."

Taking a breath, she finally turned to look at her older sister's grave. Her father stepped closer to the headstone. Anna hung back. She hadn't been out here since the day of Candace's funeral. That should have told her something, she thought.

She stood, hearing the ocean on the bluff below, smelling the sea, a breeze whispering in the tops of the tall palms nearby.

Finally she joined her father in front of Candace's headstone. "Beloved daughter and sister," the inscription read above the dates of Candace's life. Such a short life. Anna realized a day hadn't gone by that she hadn't felt guilty.

Her dad took her hand, his gaze on the gravestone. He'd been right. He'd told her she needed to come up here. Her life had somehow been all tied up with Candace's, as if she felt she had to make up for her sister's life being cut so short.

But the last few days she'd realized she couldn't bring her sister back, no matter how good she was at saving other people. This was her life and she had to start living it for herself.

She'd been afraid to marry Flint. Afraid of so many things. The SWAT training had made her feel safe. But after what had happened at city hall, she knew there was no magic bullet. Life was a gamble. All the training in the world couldn't protect her.

Nor would it have protected Candace. Nothing could protect a person from the people she loved. Nor from a broken heart. Or even worse. Nothing could make Anna safe from her fears of intimacy and motherhood and living in her older sister's shadow.

The realization that she was scared to death of being a mother surprised her. But she saw now that it was true. Her own mother had been such a disappointment to her. What if Anna was like her?

Even as the question formed, Anna knew the answer. She wasn't her mother. Nor was she her sister Emily. Or her sister Candace.

Too bad that revelation hadn't come five years ago, she thought with a wry smile as she looked down at her sister's grave. All these years she'd felt responsible for encouraging Candace to marry Darrel. Her family had failed Candace, but even if they hadn't, Anna wondered if they could have saved her sister. The other times Candace had broken up with Darrel, she'd always gone back to him. As Anna stood looking down at her sister's grave, she knew why. Candace had loved him. She hadn't been able to let go of him even when she knew she should have.

No wonder Anna had been so afraid of love.

The breeze coming up off the Pacific sighed in the palm fronds as she and her dad walked back to the car.

MAX CALLED ANNA AT HOME that night. "I've got some bad news about Lorna Sinke."

Anna held her breath. She'd just seen the woman at the hospital earlier that day. Lorna had been conscious, her condition still critical, though.

"She's dead, Anna. I'm sorry."

Anna gripped the phone, shaking her head. She'd failed. Tears stung her eyes.

Max sighed. "I don't want you blaming yourself, Anna. You did everything possible."

He knew her too well. She was mentally beating herself up because she hadn't gotten Lorna to a hospital sooner.

"If you hadn't gone in there, a lot more people would have died," he said.

But she hadn't saved the one person she'd gone in for.

"This probably isn't the best time, but I also wanted to ask you when you thought you'd be ready to come back to work," Max said. "I'll understand if you want more time…."

"I need to talk to Flint first."

CHAPTER FIFTEEN

One week later

"YOU CAN GO HOME this afternoon," the doctor announced as he came into Flint's room.

Flint thought about going home to his boat. It had been his sanctuary before Anna had come back to town. But just the thought of it now...

"Thanks, Doc." He turned to look out at the skyline. He could see a little blue of the Pacific in the distance. He wondered where Anna was.

She'd come by every day, but whenever he tried to talk about what he needed to say to her, she'd stopped him, insisting they would have time to talk once he was out of the hospital.

He turned at the sound of the room door swinging open, hoping it would be her.

"How ya feeling?" Max asked, coming into the room. "You don't have to look so disappointed to see me."

Flint laughed. "Sorry. I just thought it might be...someone else."

"Anna?" Max pulled up a chair as the doctor left. "I heard she's been by every day."

How was it that Max managed to hear so much? Flint wondered. "Doc says I can leave this afternoon."

"You need a ride out to the boat?" Max asked.

Flint shook his head. "I can drive, and I guess the team brought my car over."

Max leaned forward in the chair. "Did the doctor say when you can come back to work?"

Flint hadn't even thought about getting back to work. It surprised him. There'd been a time when all he thought about was work. But that had been to keep himself from thinking about Anna. "Six weeks before I can do much of anything."

"So you're going to be on the desk for a while," Max said thoughtfully.

The chief hadn't just stopped by to check on him, Flint realized.

"You've been through a hell of a lot," Max said. "That kind of experience can change a man."

Flint remembered how he'd felt when he'd been wounded, lying in that hallway, knowing Anna was still in there with a killer and a suicidal man with a bomb. "What is it you're trying to say?"

"Just that your priorities might be different now. Some men wouldn't be able to go into another situation like the one you just lived through."

Not if Anna was in that room, Flint thought. Was that what Max was getting at?

Max tossed an envelope next to Flint on the bed.

"What's this?" he asked as he picked it up, half afraid to open it.

"Just take a look."

Flint carefully pulled the sheets of papers out of the envelope. He frowned as he saw what they were and looked up at Max.

"It's an application for assistant chief of police of Courage Bay," Max said.

"I can see that."

"The position is opening up in the next six weeks. I thought you might be interested."

"You think I can't do my job anymore?" Flint asked.

"No, I'd put my money on you any day. I just think that you might have joined SWAT for the wrong reasons." Max held up a hand. "Don't get me wrong. You're great at your job. But I've seen men who have joined the force who are running from something, a loss of some kind. That kind of gung-ho, do-whatever-it-takes attitude gets the job done, but doesn't lead to a lifetime of happiness."

Flint knew he had been that kind of guy, so he didn't even bother to argue.

"You said a long time ago that one day you wanted to be chief of police," Max was saying.

Back when Flint had been engaged to Anna.

"Well, I have no intentions of giving up the chief of police job for a very long time, but I'd be damned proud to have you as my assistant chief, and I'd put in a good word for you with the hiring board."

Flint stared down at the papers. Wasn't this his dream just five years ago?

"You don't have to make up your mind now," Max said, getting to his feet. "I don't need your answer for a week or so. You're getting a jump on applying. Take your time." He patted Flint's shoulder. "You and Anna did one hell of a job in there the other day, Flint. I'm sure you won't be surprised when you hear about the medals the two of you will be receiving."

"We didn't do it for medals."

"That's probably why you both have so many of them," Max said, stopping at the door to smile back at Flint. "Give the future some thought."

Flint stared after him. He hadn't been able to think about anything else.

ANNA CALLED THE HOSPITAL that afternoon but Flint had already been released. When she called his home number, there was no answer. She didn't leave a message because what she had to say, she needed to say in person. She'd waited because she didn't want to have the discussion in a hospital room.

She had just hung up when the doorbell rang.

"We need to talk," Flint said when she opened the door.

She stared at him. He looked paler than he had at the hospital.

"Are you all right?" she asked, ushering him into the apartment.

"Fine."

"I thought you weren't supposed to get out of the hospital for another few days?"

He turned to look at her as she closed the door. "I'm an exemplary patient. I also heal fast, and I couldn't stand lying there any longer." His gaze softened as he seemed to search her face.

"Sit down," she said, suddenly afraid. He checked out early to come see her?

He sat down gingerly on the edge of the couch.

"Can I get you something to drink?"

He shook his head. "Anna?" He glanced past her to the rest of the apartment as if he thought he heard something. "Could you sit down?"

She nodded, too nervous to sit, but anxious to hear why he'd come here like this.

"I have to know where we go from here," he said.

She'd dreaded this day. "I have to be honest with you."

FLINT FELT HIS HEART drop, his mouth suddenly go dry. He watched her get up and walk to the deck. Beyond her he could see the Pacific, a shimmering, undulating silver backdrop.

"I've been lying to myself." She turned to look at him.

He held his breath. *Don't let her tell me she doesn't love me. I know that's a lie. But does she love me enough to give me another chance? That was the question, wasn't it?*

"I'm trying to understand what happened five years ago," she said quietly.

"Look, I was a fool. I had no right making you feel like you had to choose between a career and marriage to me."

"Flint, I knew how strongly you would feel about my being on the SWAT team before I even brought it up."

He shook his head. He could see where she was headed. But if she tried to tell him that they were all wrong for each other...

"I think I chose that career path because it was an easy way out of the relationship," Anna said.

He'd thought his heart couldn't drop any farther. He pushed himself to his feet, his gaze locking with hers. "Don't you dare try to tell me you didn't love me."

She smiled sadly and shook her head. "I'm through lying to myself. Or you. I loved you so much it scared me, Flint. I felt as if my life was spinning out of my control. It was one of the reasons I decided to join SWAT. I thought it would give me the control I'd lost."

He cocked his head at her. "But that meant leaving me."

She nodded. "You were the reason my life was out of control."

He stared at her. "So now you have your life under control again. That's what you haven't been able to tell me. You don't want me fouling it up again."

She smiled and shook her head. "The incident at city hall proved how little control we have over our lives. Those hostages probably thought they were in control when they got up that morning."

He frowned and reached to take her hand, turning the palm up and staring down at it for a moment before he planted a kiss in the center and released it.

"The day at city hall made me realize something I had been denying for five years," she said.

Finally it was coming. The real reason she'd left him. Hadn't he known all along it wasn't SWAT? It was him. She hadn't wanted to marry him.

"I love you," she said simply. "I never stopped loving you. I tried. I thought that once I had the career I needed, wanted, I would get over you. But when Max called and offered me the job, I couldn't wait to get back here. I told myself it was because this was home and that it had nothing to do with you. But that was a lie, too."

He felt his heart lift like a hot-air balloon. Did he dare hope? "Are you trying to tell me that you still love me?"

Anna nodded, tears making her eyes glisten. "Is there any way we can start over?" As she waited for his answer, she thought of everything they'd been through since the first day they met.

"We can't go back. There is no changing what has passed," he said. "We have to find a place to start again."

"Is that possible?" she asked, her heart in her throat.

"Anything is possible with you in my life," he said, his voice cracking with emotion.

She took a breath. "I was hoping we could take it slow. A lot has happened." She waved a hand through the air, but he had to know she was talking about city hall. Was it possible those hours trapped in that room had changed him, as well? "I feel like we need to sort out some things alone before we talk about a future together."

Flint nodded. Five years ago he would have seen her need for space as her wanting out of the relationship, and would have fought her tooth and nail. He couldn't have given her the space back then and they both knew it.

She waited, wondering if the two of them had changed enough over the last five years, over the last few weeks.

Flint smiled and reached out to take her hand. "Take as much time as you need. I'm not going anywhere."

Two weeks later

THE SUN GLISTENED low over the Pacific as Anna walked down the dock. She was surprised to find out Flint lived on a boat. She realized how little she knew about him. He'd never mentioned wanting to own a boat while they'd been together.

It rattled her more than she wanted to admit that she might not know Flint as well as she thought she did. Over the past two weeks he hadn't called. He'd sent a bouquet of flowers and a note saying he was there for her if she needed him. Oh, how she needed him.

Her footsteps echoed on the worn boards of the dock.

Flint's boat was a thirty-five-foot motorized trawler, blue and white, sitting in a slip at the end of the marina.

As she neared it, the sun caught on the stern. She stumbled as she read the lettering on the side. *Anna*. He'd named the boat *Anna?*

"Hello?"

She was startled to see Flint appear from below-decks. He was wearing nothing but a swimsuit, his body glistening with sweat, tanned, beautifully sculpted. He looked healthy in spite of the scars, some newer than others. Several she'd never seen before.

She stood staring at him. He looked wonderful. Her heart leaped at the mere sight of him.

"You all right?" he asked, moving across the deck to jump effortlessly down beside her. The dock swayed a little and she felt as if she didn't have her sea legs. A born surfer and she felt so off balance he had to take her arm to keep her from falling into the water between the dock and boat.

"Anna? Are you sure you're all right?"

She looked up into his face. "You named your boat *Anna*."

He nodded. "What else would I call her?"

Tears blurred her eyes. Water lapped at the sides of his boat. She shook her head.

"Would you like to see it?" he asked softly. He was still holding her arm. He gave it a playful tug and she let him help her onto the boat.

It was cool belowdecks. She felt a little better, a little more stable. She'd had a lot to think about the last three weeks, but one thing she knew soul-deep. She loved this man. She would always love this man.

"I didn't know you wanted a boat," she said, turning to look at him.

He had pulled on a shirt and was buttoning it as if he thought his lack of clothing was making her uncomfortable.

She stared at the last glimpse of chest, wanting to put her palms flat against his skin, knowing it would be warm to the touch, smooth.

"Flint." His name came out on a breath. She stepped into his arms. It was so easy that she wondered why it had taken her so long.

He wrapped his arms around her, cradling her head in one large hand as his other arm encircled her waist and pulled her closer.

His body was warm and strong. She let herself lean into him, let him take the weight from her. From deep within her came a feeling so strong, it made her catch her breath: this was where she belonged. This was where she had always belonged.

FLINT HELD HER tightly, afraid to let her go. Why had she come here? She felt so right in his arms. Did he dare hope?

She pulled back a little and looked up at him. It had been so long since he'd seen desire in her eyes....

"Anna?" It came out a whisper.

She pulled his head down to hers and kissed him, taking his breath away. He pulled her closer. Her lips parted. He kissed her, heart pounding.

"Make love to me," she whispered against his lips.

He pulled back to meet her gaze, saw that devil desire in her eyes and something more. Love.

Sweeping her up into his arms, he carried her back to the stateroom.

Her fingers worked his buttons, freeing him of his shirt as he lay beside her on the bed.

He lifted the thin cotton top she wore, pulling it over her head. Her body was as he remembered it, a little fuller, her breasts wonderfully round, filling her bra to overflowing.

He bent to free a rosy-brown nipple from the silk cup and slipped it into his mouth, her flesh warm on his tongue.

Desire rippled through him, waves of memories mixing with the Anna lying next to him now. They fought to strip each other, her need to feel his bare skin seemingly as desperate as his own.

WHEN THEY WERE FINALLY naked, Anna let out a long sigh as their bodies melded together. His lips grazed across hers, the sound of her name flowing out on a warm, soft breath.

She reveled in his touch as his fingers brushed across her flesh, sending trails of fire through her blood.

He pressed her to the mattress, his gaze meeting hers. She prayed he wouldn't speak. They had never needed words, communicating instead through touch and gazes and soft, sweet groans of pleasure.

His fingers caressed her, finding the once familiar spots, discovering new ones that spurred her desire until she was panting, her body glistening with sweat, her need for him almost more than she could stand.

She looked up at him, a plea in her eyes.

He entered her, filling her, completing her. She rocked against him, clutching at his shoulders as he drove himself deeper and deeper in her. She matched his movements, the pace picking up to a frenzy. She arched, her head thrown back as he brought her to climax and quickly followed, his cries echoing her own.

Anna lay spent in his arms, her cheek pressed against his chest, his arm around her. She could hear him breathing, hear the beat of his heart begin to slow. She closed her eyes, savoring the quiet after the storm. There were so many things she wanted to say to him.

But as she looked over at Flint lying next to her, his arm draped across her waist, she knew there would be plenty of time to talk about the past. *And* the future. Neither of them was going anywhere.

EPILOGUE

I T WAS A WARM, sunny Southern California day on the beach when Flint proposed to Anna again.

He knew in his heart that the third time really was the charm. He'd held on to the ring, but now he wondered if he should have gotten her another one, a new one for a new beginning.

"Anna," he said as she came up from the water, smiling, her surfboard under her arm, her tanned skin glistening with droplets of water. He'd never seen anything more beautiful in all his life.

She dropped onto the towel next to him, smiling, happy, completely content. He could see that all the ghosts from her past were gone. Anna had become her own woman in ways he doubted she'd dreamed possible.

They'd spent the past few weeks either at his boat or in her apartment, hardly ever apart. Neither had returned to work. Max had given them both a leave of absence.

"You know that I would never again try to stop you from doing whatever you wanted with your life," Flint had told her over and over.

She'd smiled and nodded. "I just have to decide what's right for me."

Now he turned to her, getting to one knee in the sand

as he reached into his pocket for the tiny velvet box holding the engagement ring.

She seemed to be holding her breath, her eyes wide, and for one awful moment he thought she might bolt back toward the Pacific.

"Anna," he said, and cleared his throat. "Will you marry me?"

ANNA HELD HIS GAZE for a long moment, reveling in this man she'd fallen in love with, then she looked down at the ring in the velvet jewelry box. Her heart leaped to her throat and her eyes welled with tears.

"Oh, Flint," she said. "You saved my ring."

He seemed to be holding his breath. He let out a long sigh and smiled as he reached for her hand.

She watched as he slipped the ring back on her finger. It felt so right. "I'm never taking it off again."

"Does that mean you'll marry me?"

She laughed and realized she hadn't said yes yet—and Flint was still on one knee in the sand.

She threw her arms around him. "Oh, Flint, I thought you would never ask." She laughed again and he joined her. It was a wondrous sound that drifted along the beach to a background of waves lapping at the shore. "I can't wait to marry you."

"COME ON IN," Max said as Flint opened the door to his office and stuck his head in. Max beamed at the sight of Flint and Anna together. "Congratulations."

"Thank you," Anna said. "I'm so glad you're going to be the best man."

"I wouldn't miss it," Max said.

"I've already asked him to keep the second week of June open," Flint told Anna, then turned back to Max. "Anna wants to get married on the beach. It will be small—mostly family, a few good friends."

The first time, they had planned a large, traditional wedding. This time, they both realized they didn't need that. They'd changed and now wanted a small and intimate wedding with just close friends and family.

"Please sit down." Max took his chair behind his desk again. "I wanted you both to hear the news first. The bullet that killed Lorna Sinke didn't come from either of the hostage takers' weapons."

It took Flint a moment to understand what Max was saying. "But those were the only two weapons the subjects had, other than the bomb."

Max nodded. "Kenny Reese and Lorna Sinke were wounded with the same weapon."

Flint blinked. "Kenny said he thought one of the councilmen shot him and had thrown the gun out the window, but the team searched the area…"

Max nodded. "I suspect whoever shot the two didn't throw it out the window but hid the gun in the room and retrieved it, taking it with them when they were rescued. We had no reason to search the hostages."

Flint was shaking his head. "You think this is the work of the Avenger, don't you."

"The Avenger?" Anna asked.

"Someone has been taking the law into his own hands," Flint explained. "If he doesn't think justice was done correctly, he makes sure the person gets the death penalty."

"You think that's who killed Lorna?" Anna said, clearly upset.

Max nodded. "So no matter what you did that day in city hall, you couldn't have saved Lorna. The Avenger would have gotten her at the hospital or one day after she left. She was a marked woman."

Flint couldn't believe this. "You're saying that one of the people in that room at city hall could be the Avenger."

Max nodded. "Of course we can't say for sure. We've got to run comparisons with the other deaths we've attributed to the Avenger. But there's a good chance this killing fits the pattern. From everything you've both told me and what I've learned from Councilwoman Gwendolyn Clark, Lorna Sinke was about to be fired from a job she had held for years." He glanced at Anna. "Add in what she told you about the cookies she'd brought to work that day and her animosity toward the councilwoman…"

"You think this Avenger, whoever he—or she—is, felt Lorna had escaped justice in the death of her parents," Anna said. "So without even a trial, this Avenger killed her?"

"We can't ignore that possibility." Max studied Anna closely. "I know you liked her.

"I didn't want to see her die," Anna said, thinking about the people in that city hall meeting room. "I'd put my money on Gwendolyn Clark."

"We have no proof, and we have the previous cases to consider, but I can assure you we will be keeping a close eye on all the former hostages," Max said. "By the way, that assistant chief job is yours, Flint, if you're interested." He smiled. "I assume you told your future bride that you'd applied."

"No." Flint looked over at a surprised Anna. "I was waiting until I was sure I had the job. How do you feel about being married to Courage Bay's assistant chief of police?"

Her eyes shone with tears. "I am going to love being married to you, no matter the title."

Flint hugged his future bride, anxious to hear those wedding bells ringing.

"I suppose this would be a good time to tell you, Max," Flint said. "Anna would like to stay on as your SWAT paramedic."

Max's gaze went to Anna in surprise. "You're sure. After that first day of work—"

"She's too good at what she does," Flint said.

Anna smiled. "It's only until I get pregnant, and I have to be honest with you, Max, we've decided to start a family right after the wedding. But until then…"

Max beamed. "I couldn't be happier for the two of you."

Flint recognized that smile of Max's as the chief leaned back in his chair. Was it possible Max had gotten Anna back here, hoping this would happen?

Flint met his boss's gaze and knew he owed Max a debt he would never be able to repay. He smiled. "Thanks." He looked over at Anna. She was smiling at Max, as well. If their first child was a boy, Flint was pretty sure Anna would agree that his name should be Max.

Ordinary people. Extraordinary circumstances.
Meet a new generation of heroes—
the men and women of
Courage Bay Emergency Services.
CODE RED

A new Harlequin continuity series continues
May 2005 with
CRITICAL AFFAIR
by M.J. Rodgers

Food poisoning contaminates a wedding rehearsal
dinner. The entire wedding party is rushed to E.R.
Only the bride, Jennifer Winn, is unaffected. And now
the groom is dead....

Here's a preview!

MICHAEL WATCHED JENNIFER as she stood in front of the camera, talking about the day's high temperatures and letting her viewers know that if they were going to be out tonight, they'd need sweaters because of the brisk ocean breeze.

She had a relaxed, conversational style, as though she were sitting across from her audience in her living room. And a natural warmth that people were happy to invite into their homes.

When she introduced the young girl beside her, Penelope read the barometric gauge and explained in a squeaky voice that the number had dropped over the past hour, creating a low pressure. That was the reason the southern breeze off the sea was being drawn toward Courage Bay.

Michael knew why Jennifer selected the children she did. It was one of the many things that attracted him to her.

When she ran out of his house Sunday morning, he understood that she never wanted to see him again. He fully intended to honor her wishes. But he couldn't now. And a selfish part of him was glad. For despite the reason that brought him here today, just being able to see her again made him feel like smiling.

After letting the viewers know there would be some light morning fog that would clear the beaches by noon and leave the next day full of sun, Jennifer threw it back to the news anchors. A second later, the engineer told her they were clear.

She bent down and gave her beaming co-star a warm hug. Then she headed toward her car at the far corner of the lot.

Michael was leaning against the driver's door.

Jennifer stopped short, freezing at the sight of him. After that brief moment of hesitation, she came steadily forward.

Michael had prepared himself for her anger. Tears. Being told to go away. Even being ignored. But when she finally stood in front of him, the expression on her face was calm.

"Hello, Michael."

Relief flooded through him. "You've forgiven me."

"Nothing to forgive. I was the one who…pushed things last Saturday. What happened was my fault."

He eased closer. "Does there have to be a fault?"

She retreated a step. "I didn't read chapter nineteen of your book until yesterday. I realize now that your situation is not typical. Whatever you do to…cope with the circumstances is understandable."

"Cope with the circumstances," he repeated. "Is that what you think Saturday night was for me?"

"It doesn't matter, Michael. It's over. Please let's leave it in the past. I have to be going."

She circled him, put her key in the car door.

"Jen, I need to talk to you."

"There's nothing more to say."

"It's about Russell's murder."

Her body stiffened as she faced him.

"I didn't want to tell that detective where I was Saturday night, but he gave me no choice," she said. "I'm sorry you were dragged into this."

"It's not a problem. What is a problem is the fact that Detective Batton didn't believe us."

"How do you know?"

"A friend of mine, another detective in the Courage Bay Police Department, spoke with Batton's partner."

"Am I understanding you correctly? Detective Batton doesn't think we were together Saturday night?"

"Oh, he thinks we were together. He also thinks that we murdered Russell. And he's doing his damnedest to build a case against both of us right now."

CODE RED

Ordinary People. Extraordinary Circumstances.

If you've enjoyed getting to know the men and women of California's Courage Bay Emergency Services team, Harlequin Books invites you to return to Courage Bay!

Just collect six (6) proofs of purchase from the back of six (6) different CODE RED titles and receive four (4) free CODE RED books that are not currently available in retail outlets!

Just complete the order form and send it, along with six (6) proofs of purchase from six (6) different CODE RED titles, to: CODE RED, P.O. Box 9047, Buffalo, NY 14269-9047, or P.O. Box 613, Fort Erie, Ontario L2A 5X3. (Cost of $2.00 for shipping and handling applies.)

Name (PLEASE PRINT)

Address   Apt. #

City   State/Prov.   Zip/Postal Code

093 KKA DXH7

When you return six proofs of purchase, you will receive the following titles:
RIDING THE STORM by Julie Miller   TURBULENCE by Jessica Matthews
WASHED AWAY by Carol Marinelli   HARD RAIN by Darlene Scalera

To receive your free CODE RED books (retail value $19.96), complete the above form. Mail it to us with six proofs of purchase, one of which can be found in the right-hand corner of this page. Requests must be received no later than October 31, 2005. Your set of four CODE RED books costs you only $2.00 shipping and handling. N.Y. state residents must add applicable sales tax on shipping and handling charge. Please allow 6–8 weeks for receipt of order. Offer good in Canada and U.S. only. Offer good while quantities last.

When you respond to this offer, we will also send you *Inside Romance*, a free quarterly publication, highlighting upcoming releases and promotions from Harlequin and Silhouette Books.

☐ If you do not wish to receive this free publication, please check here.

HARLEQUIN®
Makes any time special®

CODE RED
ONE PROOF OF PURCHASE
CRPOP9

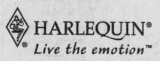

MINISERIES

Love—not-exactly-American-style!

That's Amore!

USA TODAY bestselling author

Janelle Denison

and

Tori Carrington

Leslie Kelly

For three couples planning a wedding with a little family "help," it's way too late to elope, in this humorous new collection from three favorite Harlequin authors.

Bonus Features:
Wedding Customs,
Tips & Tricks,
Funniest Wedding
Stories...
and more!

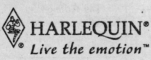

Live the emotion™